I0589148

Creative Texts Publishers, PO Box 50, Barto, PA 19504
visit www.creativetexts.com

Creative Texts Publishers products are available at special discounts for bulk purchase for sale promotions, premiums, fund-raising, and educational needs. For details, write Creative Texts Publishers, PO Box 50, Barto, PA 19504, or visit www.creativetexts.com

SCAVENGER
by Jerry D. Young
Published by Creative Texts Publishers
PO Box 50
Barto, PA 19504
www.creativetexts.com

Cover photo modified and used by license.
Credit: Augustin Ruiz

The following is a work of fiction. Any resemblance to actual names, persons, businesses, and incidents is strictly coincidental. Locations are used only in the general sense and do not represent the real place in actuality.

ISBN: 978-0-692-59035-5

SCAVENGER
By
JERRY D. YOUNG

SCAVENGER

CHAPTER ONE

Jimmy Holden grew up in a very liberal household. Despite everything his parents and other extended family, related or not, tried to get him to grow up liberal, he didn't. He wasn't right wing extremist conservative, just… conservative. He believed in the Constitution. The way it was originally written, backed up by the beliefs of the time.

When he was young he did as he was asked, working on the commune's farm with little protest. He learned then that it was approach as much as the act of doing something that made a difference.

Those in the commune lived a day to day existence. They talked about self-sufficiency, but never seemed to be self-sufficient. Many were on welfare of one type or another, and despite the rules shared what they had with the rest of the commune during tough times. And they always seemed to have bad times. They felt sharing more important than their word that they wouldn't.

Sure, that garden and small animal farm provided them with salads in the summer and some small amount of meat in the fall, but there was never enough to put up for the winter.

Many were vegetarians and even Vegans. They bought most of their food at health food stores with the income some of them produced, and what some could get on welfare.

They lived off the grid, sort of. They needed phone for internet, because the internet was the great equalizer of ideas. And they needed electricity for the computers, the co-great equalizer, to use the internet, and as a good way to buy self-sufficient things like hemp products.

Abhorrent as the thought of fur was to them, leather shoes and other products were all right. Of course they used things made of hemp when they could. When they couldn't, plastic was all right. They needed gasoline for the vehicle which they needed to transport those that had jobs to and from them. They just didn't link the use of petroleum, which killed seabirds and seals, with their use of oil based products. The oil industry yes, themselves, no.

No TV, of course. But music was good for the soul, enough so that electronic instruments were okay.

There was just inconsistency after inconsistency. The home school education was very liberal and leftist. Fortunately, Jimmy had access to a good county library and had the will to learn on his own. As he grew older, while he still bore responsibility for much of the farm operation, he also found work in town.

When he left the commune to enter the military when he was eighteen, it was the last time he was welcome there, if he was going to be a baby killer. The fact that he would be going for a business degree in college after his service was up, and then would be entering big business, an anathema to the members of the commune; put the permanence to his lack of welcome. His parents wouldn't even say good-bye to him when he left the commune to get on the bus headed for basic training.

His test scores would have let him into just about any MOS in the Army. He opted for, and was taken into, the sniper program. He'd never handled a weapon of any kind before, and learned the basics of shooting in boot camp, and the fine art aspects of it in sniper school. He was rotated into the Gulf as soon as he graduated.

Jimmy kept to himself, as much as he could, during his six years in service. Being a sniper and a true expert at all types of camouflage, including role camouflage, it wasn't hard for him to do. Even when there were other people around, he was alone with his own thoughts. Mostly thoughts of the future, and how not to live it the way his parents and their commune did.

He went into the service with five hundred dollars in his pocket from jobs he'd done, and the clothes on his back. His very nice enlistment bonus, as well as all of his pay, he put into gold and silver coins, kept in the internet 'no-records' dealer's vault. Jimmy took advantage of just about every free service the military offered, including free travel, when available. He still had over a hundred dollars of the five hundred he'd started with when he mustered out.

The military was paying his way through school. He found a decent job that paid all his living expenses, plus a bit. He had on campus housing, and got around on a Montague Paratrooper bicycle, like the ones he'd seen some of the troops use in the Gulf. It was his first big purchase since he'd left the commune.

Summers he worked a second job, acquiring more gold and silver with the money earned. He now had the gold and silver on site, cached in several places.

The college sponsored many free activities and Jimmy, as he had in the Army, took advantage of them. They provided something of a social life, as much as he wanted. He studied hard and worked hard. It didn't leave much time to play, hard or otherwise. Jimmy was still a conservative, and simply ignored the highly liberal aspects of the college during his time there, though he didn't violate the no guns rule the college had implemented.

With his military service and excellent academic record, Jimmy had no problem getting a good project manager's position with a national company when he graduated. He continued his austere lifestyle, finding an efficiency apartment within biking distance of his work. Jimmy now began the second stage of the long range plans he'd developed while still in the Army.

It was coming up on the 2016 elections, and all indications were the Democrats would go into a second four-year term of controlling both houses of congress and the presidency. The first four years, beginning in 2013, the Democrats concentrated on establishing a solid base with their supporters.

2017 was looking to be the start of very bad times for those with a conservative mind set. Plans being discussed openly now included a new, more comprehensive assault weapons ban, including restriction of person-to-person sales of weapons; open borders to the point of a new combined nation; restrictions on gold and silver ownership; a new luxury tax; and mandatory ID chip implants. Only those with implants would be entitled to certain benefits. Rumored, but not announced, was a wealth reallocation program involving the continuing changes to currency design, and eventually a total gun ban, starting with a handgun ban after the new AWB was in force.

Jimmy began to spend money like it was going out of style. Every penny that didn't feed, house, or transport him went into preparations for the upcoming political changes. Person-to-person sales of firearms were still legal in his state, so Jimmy began to attend every gun show in the state, acquiring off the record items sure to be banned or controlled in the future.

He had a feeling that a few people were starting up straw-man purchase schemes, but Jimmy didn't question the people from whom he bought, except to confirm in some way that they weren't setting him up. He was careful never to ask, or even imply, for someone to buy something over the table so he could buy it from them without paperwork.

Non papered items, like spare parts, he bought over the table, here and there, never making large purchases of any one item at any one dealer. It was the same with ammunition. He bought thousands of rounds from no-records dealers and individuals.

He turned around and sold some items to dealers, getting clear bills of sale for them, in case there were any questions in the future about his presence at the gun shows.

Having used a Barrett .50 BMG caliber sniper rifle in the Gulf, Jimmy wanted one, but was having no luck finding an un-papered one. It was the only thing on his list that didn't get marked off during 2016.

One of the other things he did get in 2016 was a good vehicle. He went shopping at the junkyard in January for parts. By December the thing was completed.

The frame came from a 2008 1-ton Chevy extended crew cab with eight-foot bed. Jimmy had the frame reinforced. The pickup originally had a diesel in it, but that had been pulled. Jimmy opted for another diesel engine, but a GM 6.5 non-electronic model.

The engine carried and drove a high capacity GM generator from a wrecked semi. Also from the same semi came an air compressor and power steering pump. A second power steering pump from another truck was mounted for use with hydraulic tools.

The air compressor and the second power steering pump had accumulators. The air conditioning pump was a new GM unit. On a custom bracket was mounted a Premier Power Welder 190 amp on-board welder.

Transmission and transfer case were the original one-ton units. Two driven steering axles and the rear steering control came from USA6x6.com. The suspension was a heavy duty air shock system, adjustable from standard stance to a six-inch lift. Everything was protected by heavy skid plates.

All lube points that didn't rotate were extended to the right front wheel well. All vents were snorkeled, as was as the air intake and the dual exhaust system, for safe fording. All wiring was placed in sealed metal conduit for water proofing, abrasion resistance, and EMP resistance. High pressure stainless steel pipe and fittings were used to run air and hydraulic power to the front and rear of the vehicle.

SCAVENGER

Three fuel tanks were custom built and installed, two along the outboard sides of the frame and one center rear of the frame. All were skid plated.

The body was made from two wrecked Suburban's. The front two thirds of one and the rear two thirds from the other. The additional length was needed for the longer wheelbase of the extended crew cab, long box pickup frame.

Under the hood, fed by the generator were three batteries, hooked up through an isolator. Two were heavy-duty starting batteries for the twenty-four-volt starter. The third battery was a heavy-duty deep cycle battery for twelve-volt power, and with the inverter installed, 120v power, too.

The original dash had been removed from the front section of one of the bodies and a custom one built, using mechanical gauges wherever possible. Simple electronic gauges were used where necessary.

Eight-way leather adjustable bucket seats were installed for driver and passenger. An identical set of seats made the Suburban a four-seater, with access to the rear of the vehicle by going between the rear seats. And there was a huge amount of cargo room in the rear section of the Suburban.

A low console was built between the front bucket seats, up to the dash. It contained the main 12-volt power feed from the batteries. All individual lighting units were routed through a series of relays and switches under the console. Switches on top of the console panel controlled the auxiliary lights.

When opened, the panel exposed more switches. They allowed the driver to activate or turn off brake lights and tail lights independently of the normal automatic switches. There were also overrides for the automatic interior lights so they wouldn't come on when the doors were opened. When folded closed the switches to override the automatic switches was hidden.

In the section of console between the switch panel and the dash, were mounted the radios the Suburban normally carried. A lift up fine copper mesh cover, coupled with the copper enclosure box protected them against EMP. There were switch controlled relays to isolate the power and antennas from the faraday cage. Another faraday cage was built into the dash in front of the passenger seat to hold a laptop computer and portable color printer.

A large GPS mapping screen was on the face of the dash above the floor console. It boasted voice activation and speech capability. Jimmy didn't bother with trying to EMP proof it.

The rear of the Suburban was accessed from outside with a custom built door system. There was a lift glass in a lift gate and split swing open lower doors.

The front bumper assembly was a shop built unit. It incorporated a spare tire carrier, hydraulic winch, 2" receiver, brush guards, light mounts, and two contoured tool boxes.

The rear bumper had a 2" receiver, swing away mounts for a spare tire and four jerry cans, and a ladder to the roof rack. The full length roof rack carried two spare tires, four remote control spot/flood lights, and additional high intensity lights, as well as the antennas for the communications gear, with plenty of room to carry additional gear.

One inside side tool box contained hydraulic and air tools, a receiver mounted hydraulic winch, and accessories for the winches. The other side tool box contained pioneer tools like shovels, pick-mattock, axe, pry bars, and Hi-Lift jack. That still left plenty of room for cargo.

The first piece of major legislation in 2013 was the new AWB, even more restrictive than the previous one. It included anything over .458 caliber in rifles and handguns, modern or antique, weapons originally designed for military use, and magazines of more than six rounds. Only the grandfather clause that was part of the original legislation was taken out, allowing current owners to keep their weapons that didn't conform to the ban, though they were strongly encouraged to turn them in 'for the good of the nation'.

Private sales were banned completely. All sales had to go through a licensed dealer and there was a twenty-five dollar transfer tax charged on all purchases, both incoming and outgoing. Sixty percent of gun dealers in the United States went out of business within two years.

Americans were once again denied the right to own gold bullion and coins. This time the ban and recall involved silver, as well. Any coinage of any nation containing gold or silver minted after 1932 had to be turned in for face value. A set buy back price of fifty-dollars per ounce of gold and two-dollars per ounce of silver was announced for bullion and non-denominated coinage.

Only numismatic gold and silver coins prior to 1932 were allowed. Any coins valued for bullion purposes had to be turned in. Making, owning, and wearing jewelry of a design created for bullion purposes was prohibited. The decision of whether or not an object was considered bullion was strictly up to a government committee.

Only paper ownership of gold and silver was allowed, such as mining and related stocks. Ownership of electronic gold and silver was also banned, as was in absentia ownership of gold and silver anywhere in the rest of the world.

Penalties were harsh for those not cooperating in the turn-in, and penalties for smuggling precious metals and guns even harsher.

In the rest of the world gold jumped to $1,500.00 an ounce, and silver $60.00 an ounce. Numismatic prices also skyrocketed.

Jimmy had obtained a concealed weapons permit as soon as he left the military, though he didn't carry on the college campus, since it was banned when he was there. He'd picked up an old, reliable Colt 1911A1 and a couple of spare magazines to use with the permit. It was the one gun he had registered. All his precious metals, guns, and related items were cached.

As he began to accumulate food, part regular packaged goods off the grocery shelves, part LTS (long term storage) food, he cached much of it, too, in environmentally controlled warehouse rooms, all over the city. There were also a couple of caches outside the city, but it was harder to find the environmentally controlled ones, which he wanted for the food storage.

Food prices were already going up, due in part, to the bad weather going into the second decade of the 21st century. Jimmy was becoming concerned that food distribution would eventually come under federal government control. There was talk of hoarding laws becoming possible in the future. Jimmy wanted LTS food purchased and cached before the companies were forced to keep long term records.

But no matter how much stored food you have, it will eventually run out. Jimmy wanted a permanent supply, or as permanent as humanly possible. Other than unlimited money, that meant he would have to have control of the source, or sources, of food. The only simple way to do that was a working farm. He began to look for one and also some farm hands, preferably a family with a couple of part time hands.

Jimmy couldn't find the ideal situation. He settled for investing in a moderate sized farm that needed capital to improve its operation. It had been inherited by two brothers and a sister, all of whom had gone to agricultural college. They knew what they wanted to do with the farm, but didn't have the means.

Jimmy liked their ideas, and gave them the money, in return for a percentage of food production for as long as the family owned the farm. One stipulation was that they began a small scale biodiesel operation, financed by Jimmy. Again, it wasn't ideal, but Jimmy decided it would have to do.

They agreed to his stipulations, including managing small herds of Black Angus cattle, American Bison, and horses that Jimmy would buy and keep at the farm for future use.

The housing market collapsed in 2014. Interest rates had skyrocketed as taxes increased under the very liberal Democratic control. Jimmy decided to take advantage of the collapse. He had great credit. Property values were decreasing and he was able to find some very good deals on land in several small towns around the city. In each he bought a large corner lot in a good neighborhood and built a quadraplex on it, with full basement, which was reserved for his use alone.

Each one filled quickly with the reasonable rental rates he was charging, since space heating, cooking, and hot water were wood fired. The income from one financed the next. Jimmy moved some of his caches to the basements as they were completed, but still kept a few of the rental storage units as caches.

2015 saw the implementation of full scale ID chip implants. More and more services required the chip to be in place before service was rendered; including medical care; welfare type benefits; Social Security benefits; buying a vehicle, property, or firearms, and several other services. By 2020 the chip would be required to buy groceries.

Jimmy decided to wait until he had to have it before he got the implant. There were penalties, but they wouldn't be severe until 2020.

The luxury tax was passed. Like the AWB, it was much more comprehensive than the previous tax. Unlike the AWB, there was a grandfather clause. Anything that came under the law, made after 2010, was subject to back taxes. That included SUV's. Jimmy's custom Suburban was exempt due to the frame manufacture date of 2008. Anything purchased after January 1st, 2015, no matter what manufacture date, was subject to the tax.

Tobacco in all its forms came under the luxury tax, running the price up to $250 a carton for the generics. A total ban would become effective in 2020.

Just before the 2016 elections the Rainbow Currency Equalization Act was passed by a narrow margin. All currency, including bank accounts, held by individuals or corporations, had to be turned in for issuance of new currency.

The issue of new currency was on a sliding scale. The more you had, the lower the rate of exchange. The range was from a ten for one exchange for those with under $10,000 in assets, to a one for ten exchange for those with over $5,000,000 in assets. Those with assets between $50,000 and $100,000 were exchanged at one for one.

Having seen the handwriting on the wall, Jimmy had been spending as he made it. He had less than eight thousand in dollars, including his bank accounts, when the exchange took place. He wound up with eighty thousand of the new dollars. Unfortunately, they quickly became worth little more than the original eight thousand.

But the euphoria of the 'disadvantaged' carried the Democrats to another Presidential term, and maintained their majority control of both houses of Congress in the 2016 elections. The huge losses of the upper classes were largely ignored. Even some large corporations had to shut their doors for lack of operating funds.

Almost all the troops overseas had been brought home and mustered out. The US forces were at a fifty-year low.

Handguns were banned in 2017, except for on duty active duty law enforcement, active duty military, and special permit holders. Standard concealed weapons permits didn't qualify.

Things might have gone differently had the ban not been applied to off duty and retired police officers, and veterans. They were the first to revolt and begin to fight the attempts of confiscation. Many police, subject to the ban when off duty, refused to turn in their private weapons. They were arrested by the new BATFEPM (Bureau of alcohol, tobacco, firearms, explosives, and precious metals.).

Thousands of officers across the nation quit their forces and began an active resistance campaign. When it became obvious to the White House and Congress that the ban was not going well, additional teams of BATFEPM agents were organized with very liberal engagement rules. Gun battles erupted all across the nation as gun owners fought the confiscation.

Congress hurriedly extended the ban to all firearms in an attempt to control the rebellion. It only made it worse. There was open warfare whenever a BATFEPM team entered an area. The military and police forces had been the first be chipped. Those not actively supporting the ban became subject to restrictions on purchasing food and fuel.

There was a huge outcry, but it made no difference. The administration was determined to disarm the American population. More BATFEPM teams were hired and trained. During the first stages of the rebellion, Jimmy kept a low profile. Lower than normal. He debated what he was going to do. He made preparations. Things would have been simpler if he'd just turned in the Colt and permit. It just galled him when he thought about doing it.

The Jack Boots seemed to prefer striking at home, in the early evening hours. They didn't like witnesses, Jimmy decided. Media had learned their lesson the hard way. They didn't even try to cover gun confiscations. From the information he had been able to gather, the little guys were Jack Boots' week day duties. The big timers got hit on Saturday nights.

SCAVENGER

Jimmy got into the habit of being elsewhere during those times of day during the week days. Just sort of hanging out, unobtrusively, where he could keep an eye on the front doors of the apartment building, and the street outside. Twice he saw the Jack Boots park outside and enter the building. They had gone to using nondescript vehicles to avoid ambushes, but Jimmy could spot them easily. He made himself scarce each time.

Both times the BATFEPM agents called in the coroner. The suspects had been killed resisting arrest. The third time it happened and Jimmy was on his way back, he immediately noticed that the feds were still around. Apparently the suspect wasn't home. That meant it could be Jimmy that they were after.

He decided on the spur of the moment to make a stand. If they wanted his gun, they would have to kill him. Which was likely. The BATFEPM had some of the best weapons around. The same couldn't be said of the people. The agency was trolling the bottom of the barrel to get agents.

Using his skills as a sniper in MOUT conditions, Jimmy sneaked up on the Ryder van the BATFEPM was using. Two officers were inside. One in the cab, one in the back, with the door open a fraction. Red light was visible through the slight opening when Jimmy took a quick look. What he saw cemented his decision. He pulled a black balaclava from his rear pocket and slipped it on, then did the same with thin leather gloves from his other back pocket.

He closed the partially open door and flipped the locking mechanism in place. It was a few seconds, but then holes began to appear in the doors as the officer inside opened up with a full auto weapon of some sort.

Jimmy was already at the cab of the truck, his Colt in hand. "This is a hijack." The officer tried to draw his sidearm and Jimmy shot him in the forehead, through the open window, killing him instantly. Jimmy opened the cab door and dragged the dead man out, and climbed in. He started the engine and drove off as the rest of the BATFEPM team came storming out of the apartment building.

More fire was coming from the inside of the box and the team opened fire. The firing from inside stopped. Jimmy knew his way around the area very well. He made several turns and was then on a side street. There was a building under construction, though stopped now, with two cargo trucks there, though they were not Ryder's. Jimmy pulled alongside the other two trucks and hopped out of the cab. It was very dark where he was. After a few moments of letting his eyes adjust, Jimmy went around to the back of the truck.

There was blood dripping from a series of bullet holes right around the point where the locking bar was. Colt in hand, Jimmy opened the door slightly. The officer inside lay dead right at the doors. Though his armor had stopped many rounds that his fellow officers had fired, the three that found his head had been more than enough to kill him.

Jimmy avoided the blood as he climbed into the box van. Working quickly, Jimmy removed the things he wanted from the truck and took them to the partially completed building. He hid everything under some of the construction materials. He locked the back of the truck again, got back into the cab and moved the truck, using back streets, well away from the construction site.

After that Jimmy walked to one of his cache points in the city. There he changed out the barrel and slide of the Colt for another set. That done, he got out a sleeping bag and went to bed. When he got up the next morning he put on different clothes, and found a local service station so he could go to the bathroom.

Hailing a cab, he went to the central police station and turned himself in to the desk sergeant, setting the Colt, the three magazines, and his permit on the desk. The sergeant started to draw his gun, but Jimmy was already talking.

"I want to turn this in before the feds kill me," he said. "They were at my apartment last night and I got scared and…"

"Hold it! Hold it!" the sergeant said, raising one hand. He moved the Colt out of Jimmy's reach. "Let me get a detective to talk to you." When he picked up the permit and saw the name, he did draw his gun. "There is a federal warrant out for you! Says you killed two agents and stole their equipment van, using illegal weapons"

"What!" Jimmy exclaimed. "That's the only weapon I have. And I'm turning it in."

"Someone else has to sort this out." The sergeant looked around, leaned a bit closer and whispered, "Look, buddy, I sympathize with you, but you are in big trouble. If you walk out of here right now, I'll never say a word."

"I didn't do anything wrong. I want this cleared up. But I sure don't want to get killed by the BATFEPM."

"Hey, Lou!" the sergeant called toward another of the men working the front area of the station. People were beginning to stare. "Get Donahue! We have a live one here."

When the detective came out, the sergeant explained what Jimmy had told him. "Have you read him his rights?"

The sergeant shook his head. "Well, read them to him, and get him in a cell. Suspicion of Murder. I'll go see what I can find out."

Jimmy was booked and taken to a holding cell. A few minutes later Detective Donahue had him moved to interrogation. Jimmy went inside, followed by the detective. "Okay, Slick. What's your story?"

"Just what I told the sergeant, Detective," Jimmy said. "I'm afraid of the Jack Boots. I should have turned in the gun earlier, but I couldn't find it for a while, and now, with what is happening… I just think it is better to get rid of it."

"They're saying you ambushed them."

"How could I ambush them? I only have that Colt and it's old. They wear armor and there are several of them that come at you all at once. I've seen them in my apartment building before. No one in their right mind would ambush them. They can't have any evidence, since I didn't do it."

Detective Donahue frowned. "I'm not sure that will make them that much difference. One of their own is supposed to be here in a few minutes to pick you up."

The door to the interrogation room opened and a man in a dark blue suit entered. "Is he ready to go?" the man asked.

"Not quite yet," said Detective Donahue. "We have him under arrest for Murder."

"It's a federal warrant. Do the paperwork. I want him ready in an hour or heads are going to roll. Probably yours. You look the type to carry off duty."

Detective Donahue flushed. "I follow the law, like it or not. We're cleaning up a lot of the messes you BATFEPM guys leave behind. I'm not so sure you guys are following your own rules. This is still America. People have rights."

"Not to own a gun. Not anymore. Who is your superior?"

The detective told the agent.

"I suggest you start on that paperwork right now, Detective." He turned and stormed out of the door.

"I don't know what I can do for ya', Slick. Except keep an eye on the case. Good luck." The detective motioned at the one-way mirror and an officer came in almost immediately. "Get him ready for transfer to the feds."

"We have to?" asked the officer.

"We have to. Whether we like it or not."

Jimmy went along quietly. It was not going as well as he hoped. As the BATFEPM agent escorted him out of the station, Jimmy saw Donahue talking to several reporters. They turned and looked at him and the agent.

None too gently the agent pushed Jimmy into the back seat of the car. There was another agent standing beside it. He held three evidence bags in his hand. One contained the Colt, one the three magazines and the third Jimmy's CCW permit. Both men got into the car and they headed for the Federal Building.

Jimmy was taken to another interrogation cell. The first BATFEPM agent was joined by another. "Okay, Smiley," said the second agent. "I'm Agent

Miller. We have your gun, you dope. It's the same make and model as the one used in the murder of the box van driver and back up agent."

Jimmy almost messed up then. He started to tell them that their own men had killed the agent in the back of the box van. He shook his head. "It may be the same make and model, but it wasn't my gun. I had it on me, planning to take it to the police this morning, but I saw you guys enter the building and I got scared. I didn't even see the BATFEPM van."

"You trying to tell us that you missed seeing a great big yellow Ryder van?"

"Ryder van? Sure I saw a Ryder van. I thought someone was moving out. Don't you have your own marked vans? I've seen them before."

"Never you mind what we use in our work, Smart Guy," said the first agent, rather sharply.

"Sorry," Jimmy muttered, his head going down.

Another agent, this one female, came into the room and handed a file folder to Agent Miller.

After looking at it for long moments he handed it to the first agent, and then addressed Jimmy. "Okay, Wise Guy. Says here you were a sniper in the Army. Our driver was shot at close range, right in the forehead. That calls for some skill."

"I probably have the skill with a rifle. I doubt it with a pistol, even close up."

"Where are the rest of your guns?" the first agent asked. "We searched your apartment and came up empty."

"The Colt is the only one I have," Jimmy replied calmly.

"Had," the first agent said. "It is no longer yours."

The same female agent came into the room with another file. When Agent Miller looked at it he exclaimed, "What! Are they sure about this? And the serial numbers match?" he asked the female agent.

She shrugged. "You know they are seldom wrong."

"Okay, Ace," Agent Miller said, "You've caught a lucky break. The ballistics don't match your gun."

"I told you that…"

"Shut up! They may not match, but you're on our list now. I'd walk the straight and narrow. We'll be watching. Get him out of my sight." Agent Miller stormed out.

Rather joyfully, Jimmy thought, the first agent said, "You just made an enemy. A bad one."

"I wasn't trying…"

"Shut up."

Thirty minutes later Jimmy was out of the federal building, without having been chipped. The Feds assumed that the city police had done it when he was arrested, which was SOP. But the city police hadn't had him long enough to chip him. His military POW training had taken him through the interrogation processes with flying colors.

Jimmy went on with life as usual, except for one very quick stop at the abandoned building project one black, rainy, Sunday night to recover the items he'd stashed there. Different items went to different storage rooms around the city.

Crime rates began to jump drastically in the cities that were supposed to be the showcases of civilian disarmament. Soon the crime statistics were no longer released. Disarmament continued in the cities, but in the rural regions of the US, the BATFEPM losses began to mount to the point they were having trouble getting even bully-boys to work there.

Jimmy let it be known at work and elsewhere that the arrest had taken a lot out of him and he needed to get away for a while. It was no problem getting a six-month leave of absence from the company where he worked. He went out to the farm and re-familiarized himself with farm life for a few weeks.

While he was there he found a wrecked long wheel base truck the same year as the bodies of the Suburban. He paid the wrecking yard to build a trailer out of it. The same company that made the fuel tanks for the Suburban, made four fuel tanks for the trailer. The outside-the-rail tanks were somewhat shorter than those on the Suburban, but the under bed spare tire location tank was the same as that on the Suburban. In addition, since there was no driveline, a between-the-rails tank was added in front of the differential.

The same type of rear bumper was added that the Suburban had, including the ladder to the rack on the matching heavy-duty bed cap, the swing away spare tire and Jerry can racks, and the receiver hitch. The cap had with full opening long side windows and rear lift up door.

The front of the frame, where it began to bend to came to the hitch point had a rack built to carry a second spare, two HD deep cycle batteries, and two forty-pound propane tanks.

The Suburban was more than capable of reaching some very far off the beaten path locations, even with the trailer. He studied some internet maps and found what he wanted.

Then he bought some camping equipment and headed for the hills for a while. Or so it appeared.

Jimmy did set up camp and lived there for two weeks. Then he loaded up everything and headed back to the city.

But he didn't go back the way he'd come in. He forded the stream where he was camping, and drove the Suburban and trailer through the woods until he hit the fire road for which he was looking. The fire road took him to a county road, it to a state road, and finally to a small town where he already had a storage room, and the basement of one of the quadraplexes he owned.

Jimmy rented another storage unit, backed the trailer in and unhooked it, then backed the Suburban in beside it. He changed his appearance, closed the door, and headed for downtown on foot, with a duffle bag strapped to his back.

It didn't take long to find a used car lot. He paid $500.00 cash for a beat up junker that had just been turned in on one of those 'if-you-can-get-it-here' trade-in deals. He left the lot, fueled the little Toyota, and stopped at a handy location to change his appearance once again. Then, with a slight smile on his face, Jimmy Holden started a solo war against the federal government.

CHAPTER TWO

Using his left hand, Jimmy laboriously hand printed, on yellow tablet paper from a convenience store, with a pen from the same convenience store, his declaration of war. He took it to Kinko's and made a hundred copies on the self-serve machine.

Then he continued his journey to Chicago, a major anti-gun city, with lots of BATFEPM agents. He took a week to scout the area, using different role camouflage each day. When he had his spots picked he dropped off copies of his Declaration at each newspaper, TV station, and radio station. He then went and set up the scoped and suppressed Barrett Light Fifty that had been in the BATFEPM van and waited. When he had his chance he fired all ten rounds in the Barrett magazine.

Calmly he broke the gun down, replaced it in its case, slipped the case into the duffle bag, and swung it to his back. He was gone in minutes, headed back to the small town to switch vehicles and go back to his camp.

Agent Miller showed up three days after Jimmy returned to his camp. Jimmy thought Agent Miller's hand was twitching toward his pistol. "How long have you been here?"

Jimmy told him the first day he'd arrived. "Why?"

"We're investigating a series of murders in Chicago. You've been here all that time?"

"Sure. Just been enjoying being away from the city. Why do you think I have anything to do with murders in Chicago?"

"I'll ask the questions. You used a Barrett fifty-caliber sniper rifle in Iraq, didn't you?"

Jimmy nodded.

"You know they are illegal to own now."

Again Jimmy nodded.

"Do you own one?"

With a chuckle Jimmy replied. "No. I do not own a fifty caliber weapon. The only weapon I had you have now."

"When do you plan to leave?"

"Now is a good time, I think. To be honest, you have kind of ruined things up here for me. It isn't long before I have to go to work again, anyway."

"You are awful sure of yourself, Smart Guy."

"It's easy when you have right on your side."

"Right? Right like the great Second Amendment right?"

"No. The 'I'm innocent' right. More questions?"

"If I find out you've been lying to me, things will go hard for you."

"I understand," Jimmy said. He turned away and began to pack up his camp.

"I think you're lying and I'm going to prove it. What is down that way?"

"I don't suggest you go down there. It's a mess. I thought about it, but chickened out. That's why I'm camping here."

"We'll see," Miller said. "We know you didn't go out the way you came in. But if I can get through, that means you could, too."

"If you go, you'll see my tracks where I tried."

Miller went back to his Ford Excursion and followed the obvious tracks that Jimmy had made sure to leave, just in case. Jimmy pulled him out four hours later, hooked the trailer back up, and headed for home, a fuming Miller leading the way.

The Chicago killings seemed to galvanize the nation. It couldn't be kept off the news. It had happened in full daylight, middle of the week, with hundreds of witnesses. The Chicago papers, radio stations, and TV stations all had copies of his Declaration.

The BATFEPM began to run into even more resistance than before. Ambushes, sniping attacks, an all manner of active resistance when trying to confiscate. Dozens of people died, including women and children as the BATFEPM began to go in shooting, in response to the attacks. Attempts to quash the news coverage began to fail.

With more coverage of the BATFEPM killings, many of the news outlets began to investigate other news stories they had been warned to stay away from. News of other abuses was disseminated.

People began to protest the ID chip implants as more and more security measures were instituted in response to the violence. Travel was heavily restricted as pockets of resistance were identified. Only those with the chip could travel more than twenty-five miles from their home. People living further than that from their work required special programming in their chip to pass the check points.

In addition to the attacks on authority figures, the BATEFPM and security police, strong supporters of the various measures began to be attacked openly. There were calls to employ the military in protecting members of the Executive Branch, the Judicial Branch, and more importantly, the Legislative Branch of the government, particularly members of Congress that had supported, and were still supporting the various restrictive aspects of American life. Several had been killed. Almost all had been attacked in one way or another at least once.

The country was in an uproar. The President declared martial law and suspended the Constitution. Open warfare erupted. The President called on the UN for assistance to put down the rebellion.

Rogue elements of the US Navy shot down the first seven plane loads of Peacekeepers headed for the country. Marines from Quantico stormed the UN complex and commandeered aircraft to transport delegates and workers out of the United States. Elements of the Air Force destroyed the buildings.

Many units of the various Armed Forces were now sitting ready to do battle with their own forces.

Fearful of an attack on Washington, DC`, the President, Vice President, and key members of Congress boarded Air Force One for a flight to Geneva, Switzerland, to continue pursuing a UN solution. One of the F-15 escort pilots activated his weapons systems and shot down the plane. He was in turned destroyed by another of the escort planes, but Air Force One went down with total loss of life.

That act broke the back of the Democratic Party, which had been running into problems anyway, as the draconian measures they had begun using began to severely affect their own constituents.

The Secretary of State was sworn in as President. He was a Democrat, but a very moderate one. He immediately called for peace among Americans, restricted the BATEFPM duties for an indefinite period of time, and rescinded all the recent restrictive laws by executive order.

Agent Miller went berserk and went after Jimmy. As soon as the restrictions of gun ownership had been rescinded, Jimmy had brought out a couple of his cached firearms. A sympathetic BATFEPM agent contacted Jimmy and warned him that Miller was going after him. Jimmy smiled slightly and hung up the telephone.

Jimmy waited for Miller on the street in front of Jimmy's apartment building. It was over in seconds. Jimmy dove to his left as soon as he saw Miller approach. Miller drew and began firing. Jimmy drew his Para-Ordnance and put three quick rounds into Miller's face, dropping him almost instantly. No charges were filed, with two dozen witnesses substantiating Jimmy's statement that Miller had drawn first, without warning, and fired at Jimmy.

Even with most of the restrictions lifted, serious damage had been done to the United States economy. That, in conjunction with the continuing droughts blamed on Global Warming, the food supply became critical. You can't eat guns, or gold, or yachts, or SUV's. You can eat tobacco, but it isn't very filling. The remainder of Congress couldn't come up with a plan to resolve the shortages.

The whole world was suffering from Global Warming. Where there weren't ongoing droughts, there were monsoonal rains. Crop production per capita was at a two-hundred year low.

The US economy was in ruins due to the Rainbow Currency Equalization Act. Gold and silver began climbing again as Americans could again own it and now many wanted it badly.

The split in the military was slow in healing. There were those that had supported Presidential authority, despite the Constitution, who were still at odds with those that supported direct Constitutional authority, despite Presidential authority.

With the US having pulled back its influences from around the world, except for Israel, many countries around the world began programs of adventurism, including Spain, France, Russia, China, and Germany, in search for diminishing resources, especially food crops.

The Mid-East was at war with itself. With the nuclear umbrella protecting Israel, many of the other countries in the area began small internecine wars to try to bring back one of the many previous dynasties that had controlled the area in the past, with the stated intention of becoming strong enough to take on Israel, even if Israel continued to have US help.

The UN, now meeting in The Hague, was essentially powerless. The nations of Africa and South and Central America began fighting one another, and the incursions of the nations on their new path of adventurism.

Local communities began cracking down on illegal immigration, and the courts were letting them. Between losing benefits in many places and the much tougher economy, many Mexicans and Central Americans began to leave the US voluntarily. The streets of the US were no longer paved in gold for illegal immigrants or for natural born citizens, when it came to that.

The corporation Jimmy worked for had held on for as long as it could. It finally had to downsize and Jimmy's position was eliminated. While he job hunted Jimmy moved out to the farm, living in a small travel trailer he bought used. He helped around the farm when he wasn't out on interviews.

He installed satellite TV and satellite internet service in the trailer to keep up on the news. It wasn't good, despite the upswing in Republican popularity. Things seemed to be moving in the right direction, but the pendulum swung slowly, which Jimmy decided was probably a good thing.

New programs were developed, similar to many of the Depression Era federal works projects, without quite as much socialism involved. It was announced that the military would be rebuilding, to counter some of the activities going on in the world.

It was debated in later decades whether or not that announcement of the rebuilding program was the actual trigger, or not, but global nuclear war erupted two days after the announcement. Russia launched first, quickly followed by China. But the US was still the most powerful nation on the planet. The President released the nuclear arsenal and the US retaliated in kind. Most of the world was spared the initial effects, with only the three nations using their nuclear arsenals, targeting each other.

SCAVENGER

In the long term, however, the entire world suffered. Global warming was reversed in a few days and a new minor Ice Age began.

Jimmy was at the farm when the attack came. He sheltered with the family, in the basement of the new monolithic dome barn that had been part of the upgrade to the farm. Besides Jimmy, most of the owner's extended family came to the shelter, too. They were somewhat west of any targets, and well east of the targets to their west. They received only marginal fallout and were out of the shelter in ten days.

It was already fall, and with the overcast caused by the nuclear war, winter was going to come early. They prepped the farm for the following spring, scraping and discarding the top three inches of top soil of their fields. Jimmy helped where he could, mostly with the animals, while the others used their diesel powered equipment. Most of it was very good equipment, but far from new. Most items survived the EMP. While there were some losses to the EMP, none were critical.

They settled in to hibernate the winter, secure in food and fuel. Jimmy had retrieved more of his cached weapons and armed those over fifteen years of age at the farm. He did some basic training, and set up a few fixed defensive positions, with a watch kept on the main entry to the farm at all times.

It was well they did. In January several people tried to get onto the farm, searching for food. They were met with force. The family was prepared to help their neighbors, and had small handouts ready for distribution. It only seemed to madden the people. They left with the food, but came back during the middle of a snow storm for more.

Jimmy's long range sniper skills weren't of much use in the heavy fall of snow, but his ability to blend into the surroundings was. He went out in snow camouflage over body armor during the attack. He was able to break the back of the attack, sneaking up on and taking out three of those doing the most firing at the house. Through the swirling snow he saw several of the others begin to run away. He fired the PTR-91 until he couldn't see anyone.

They left the bodies where they lay for three days, and then Jimmy and the oldest brother, Frank, both in armor and camouflage, went out, in yet another snow storm, to make sure no one was lurking around. They moved the bodies and stripped them, recovering some useable gear. The bodies were wrapped in plastic and put in a metal storage building for burial when the ground thawed.

There were several more people that came to the farm for food, but only one more group was aggressive. When they foolishly made threats, standing right there in a group, all heavily armed, Jimmy didn't hesitate. He opened fire. When he did, several other members of the family did as well. They added the bodies to those already in the metal building.

Jimmy back tracked their approach. He didn't find any signs of any others, but he did find four vehicles, including three diesel crew cab Dodge dualies, with trailers, loaded to the gills, and a ten wheeler tanker truck nearly full of diesel.

He drove one of the vehicles to the farm and took three others from the farm back to recover the rest of the vehicles. The Dodges only had a few miles on them. Jimmy assumed they'd been liberated from a dealership. It didn't matter. They were the farms now.

SCAVENGER

As he had before, Jimmy took a share of the spoils of war, letting the farm have all four vehicles, while he took a large share of the supplies and a few of the weapons.

Those on the farm were now well equipped tactically and trained to handle emergencies. Jimmy decided to go check on his property holdings. He loaded up the Suburban and trailer and set off.

It took him a few days to get to the first small town. There were people moving about, but not that many. Checking his radiation meter, Jimmy decided a quick visual on the quadraplex would be adequate. The radiation in the area was still over 1.0R/hr.

The quadraplex was on what had been a quiet side street. It didn't look like any snow had been removed since it had started the previous fall. Jimmy turned around and left the small town. He'd check during the summer months when he could get to it without leaving the Suburban vulnerable.

So far, the people he met were civil enough, if not necessarily friendly. People seemed to want to keep what was in their area, for their own use. He was warned repeatedly not to try to scavenge in 'their' area.

Figuring the snow would be less the further south he went, Jimmy turned the Suburban in that direction, headed for another of the towns where he had a quadraplex. There was, indeed, less snow, but there was still snow. Plenty of it. When he ran into roadblocks, natural or manmade, he went around them where he could. When he couldn't he backtracked 'til he could take a different route.

Going solo had serious drawbacks. Jimmy always stopped well before dark, fixed a hot meal and then found a remote place to stay the night. He slept in a *Slumberjack* two-bag sleep system, in a trough of sorts in the equipment in the back of the Suburban. Despite the sub-zero cold at nights, he slept warmly. He never had trouble starting the Suburban after one of the cold nights.

He made it to the second quadraplex. It was intact, but deserted. The door to one of the units was open, and there were signs of rodents and other small animals inside. He checked the freestanding four door garage. There were no vehicles inside. He backed the trailer into one of the slots and the Suburban in another and began to clean up the infested unit. He stayed there three days and didn't see a soul.

Jimmy checked the outside access to the basement. It was still well concealed under three inches of earth, plus the snow. He didn't bother it. He did open one of the secret entrances located in the floor of each master bedroom in the quadraplex. He climbed down the ladder and took a look around. Everything was just as he'd left it when the quadraplex had been built. After climbing back out, he closed the hatch.

At the next small town on the southern route, Jimmy found he still had tenants. They weren't too happy that he still wanted rent.

"Look," Jimmy told the three head of households of the three units that were occupied, "It's still my property. I'm not going to kick you out in the cold. You being here helps protect this property. But I do expect some compensation. Excess food, gold or silver, of course. Firewood, anything of value. I don't ask much. A tenth ounce of gold per month or what it would buy. Let it accumulate. I'll be by once or twice a year to collect. Nothing on this trip."

Two agreed, if somewhat reluctantly. The third man angrily said, "I may just leave and burn this place to the ground."

The other two gasped in shock.

Jimmy smiled that little smile of his and replied. "If this place burns, I will find you and kill you with no mercy. I've killed before, I can do it again."

The man blanched, and looked down at his feet. "You'll get your bloody tribute!" The anger was obvious. He turned around and went into his unit of the quadraplex.

Jimmy turned to the other two men. "Any one that wants the fourth unit, the same situation goes. Let them know they will owe from the time they take up residency. If you want, you can combine resources and pay as a group."

The two nodded and Jimmy got back into the Suburban and left. There had been no indications that the tenants had found the basement and its cache.

The fourth quadraplex had burned, at least partially. It was no problem to get into the basement through the bedroom of the part that hadn't burned. He cleaned out the cache and loaded it into the trailer. The only thing he left behind was the water from the 15-gallon barrels he used for water storage.

At the fifth quadraplex there were six families using the four units. He gave them the same offer to pay to continue to stay. They seemed much less reluctant and agreed quickly, and even offered a cord of firewood in payment then and there. Jimmy declined, smiled, and shook hands all around. He'd see in a few months if they would actually pay up.

Those in the sixth quadraplex ran him off at gun point. From the looks of the weapons they brandished, they hadn't discovered the cache in the basement, if they'd even found the basement. It wasn't worth the trouble at the moment to find out. They didn't look to be a very healthy bunch.

Jimmy decided to wait until summer before he went into the city to check on the storage room caches. On the way back to the farm, he still had plenty of fuel, but he ran across a diesel tanker that still had fuel. He filled his tanks and continued, making a note of the location of the truck. He'd get someone from the farm to bring him to it so he could take it in.

He made it back to the farm without further incident. He'd kept the shortwave receiver in the Suburban on most of the time. He'd heard nothing about any government activity the entire time he was gone, though there were Amateur Radio Operators on the air. Quite a few of them.

Those on the farm had not been idle while Jimmy was gone. The farm boasted a couple of additional tractors, several more head of stock, five more running vehicles, and an even dozen semi-trailers of supplies they'd found on the roads and accumulated from abandoned farms and businesses in the area. There was even a large generator equipped Class-A motorhome that had been recovered, specifically for Jimmy's use when he was on the farm.

Jimmy settled in at the farm and waited until summer. It was a long time coming. It was a mild one, but the snow did melt away in the area by June. What field crops that could be, were planted. But the farm boasted two green houses, again part of the updating of the farm that Jimmy had financed. They were providing fresh garden produce year round, under grow lights powered by generators fueled with the biodiesel produced on the farm.

Many acres of oil crops were planted on adjacent, abandoned land. The yields were going to be low, due to the weather, so they needed as much production as they could get. Jimmy helped with the spring planting and birthing then got the itch to travel again.

He wanted to check the two quadraplexes and storage rooms he had not been able to on his first run. He hit the first town and, without the snow, was able to get to the quadraplex with no problems. It was trashed. And the residents had found the basement. When the sewer line quit working, instead of building an outhouse, or using chemical toilets, the people living there had just knocked the drain pipe loose and let the waste run into the basement. The people apparently left when the conditions got too bad.

Jimmy almost left the cache behind. Instead, he made a run into the city, checked two of the caches and recovered the contents. Then he found a dive shop. With dry suit diving gear, Jimmy went back to the quadraplex. Donning the dry suit, strapping on one of the tanks of air, and putting on the dive mask, he went into the basement and began to recover the cache. It took a while. He had to be careful to keep everything out of the foot and a half of waste in the basement. But finally the job was done.

He'd set out several five-gallon buckets of water and washed off the dry suit enough to get it off without contaminating himself in the process. The suit he threw away. He had three more. The tanks and other gear he kept. There was a small dive compressor in the trailer he'd got at the dive shop.

He went back to the farm. They were accustomed to him taking the utility tractor with backhoe and disappearing into the woods surrounding the farm when he came back from his jaunts. They knew he was caching things, but made no effort to get into them. The members of the extended farm family considered him their savior. All were sure they would not have survived the war and its aftermath without his involvement in the farm.

Some of the unattached women at the farm tried to get him to settle down with one of them, but Jimmy maintained his solo lifestyle.

The winter of 2018/2019 came early, as had the last one. And it was fierce. The planet continued to cool, and the high northern latitudes, as well as the southern tips of Africa and South America began to glaciate.

With already three feet on snow on the ground in November, three of the families to which the farm had been supplying food, showed up, lock stock and barrel, asking to stay for the winter, knowing they didn't have enough supplies to make it on their own.

There were family relationships with all three families with the extended farm family. The fourteen people and their belongings were merged with those already at the farm. It was too late to try to get any additional housing set up. The overflow went into the barn, which was near full anyway, with the additional livestock the families had brought with them.

Jimmy kept to his motorhome, mostly because he wanted to, but partly because snow accumulation was on the order of eight feet. It was too much work for Jimmy to do more than just clear space around the motorhome. Three hundred feet of near tunnel from the motorhome to the barn was too hard to keep open.

The farmers were kept busy keeping the greenhouses clear of snow. Jimmy had run an intercom cable on the ground from the motorhome to the barn, in anticipation of the heavy snow. He was able to communicate with people when he wanted to do so, which wasn't often. He didn't mention the set of snowshoes he had.

The women of the farm insisted that the path be opened the day before Christmas so Jimmy could join the celebration. Fearing it could cause a rift between him and families, or at least cause some very hurt feelings Jimmy acquiesced and began digging from his end.

He spent Christmas day with the farm families, accepting the small gifts that several people had made for him. The fact that he had nothing in return to give seemed not to make any difference at all. If anything, it enhanced the charitable feelings people felt for him. He stayed late, but insisted on going back to the motorhome after the huge evening meal.

Feeling more contented than he had in years, Jimmy fell asleep on the sofa in the living room area of the motorhome, the image of the very pregnant Lucy MacAtee sitting alone in front of the fireplace in the ranch house flashing across his memory. She was one of those from the new families.

Where Thanksgiving and Christmas had been joyful events, considering the circumstances, New Year's Day of 2019 was somber. Lucy MacAtee lost her baby on New Year's Eve. Rumors spread quickly that the baby had been badly malformed, a mutation.

People had quit worrying about it much earlier, as several babies were born quite normal after the war.

Lucy was kept isolated for several days, but she was insisting she was all right. As soon as the guard of those tending her was dropped, she bolted, going out into dark, freezing weather, during another snow storm.

As soon as he was informed, Jimmy joined the search for her. The snow had crusted over and would support very light people, which Lucy was. Not so most of the searchers. Jimmy strapped on his snowshoes and went out. As the others hunted in other directions, Jimmy had a hunch and headed for the farm's small graveyard.

He found Lucy kneeling down on the snow, above where the cemetery was. The hood of her heavy winter cape hid her face for a few moments, but then she looked up when the path of light from Jimmy's flashlight crossed her vision.

"I don't want to go back," she said. "I just want to die."

"It's not my call," Jimmy said just as quietly. "The families want you alive. I have a responsibility to them. I won't let you die out here."

Lucy didn't question how he would prevent it, but she seemed to accept it. She stood up. "I don't want to go back to the house now."

"Not a problem. I prefer the barn myself."

"Not the barn. I want to be alone for a while."

"But there's only…" Lucy sagged against him.

Half carrying her, half helping her walk, Jimmy got her back to the motorhome and inside. He keyed his radio and told the other searchers he had her, safe, at the motorhome. Several people offered to come take her to the house.

"She refuses," Jimmy said.

A couple of women fought their way across the remains of the Christmas path to the motor home to tend to Lucy. Jimmy made himself scarce, to allow the women a chance to get Lucy to go back to the house, or at least, the barn. One of them came to him and said, "She just refuses to go. We'll have to get a couple of men to come carry her back."

Lucy's voice wasn't too strong, but Jimmy heard her when she called to him, "You know what it is to want to be alone. That's all I want."

Jimmy sighed. "Let her stay here. I don't use the back bedroom, except for storage. Give me a minute and I'll get it ready."

"I don't know," the woman said. "It is such an imposition on you. We all know you like your privacy."

"Maybe that's what she needs," Jimmy said his voice low. "One of you can stay here and keep an eye on her. Help her if she has problems."

"That's just more intrusion…"

"Don't worry about it." Jimmy grinned. "Maybe the dishes will get done."

"Well, let me talk it over with Martha."

Jimmy went past the two women and rearranged the rear bedroom while they talked. Lucy was still wearing her winter cape, her eyes on her feet as she sat on the sofa.

Jimmy let the women know the room was ready. They seemed to still be discussing it, but Lucy got up and walked past them in the narrow hallway, and entered the bedroom, closing the door behind her.

Martha and Joan shook their heads.

"I think the decision had been made," Jimmy said. He went into the side bedroom and closed the door.

When he got up during the night to go to the bathroom, he saw Martha napping on the sofa, the lights down low. He looked over at the other bedroom door. It was still closed. When he got up the next morning Martha was fixing breakfast. And the dishes from the previous meal were, in fact, done.

Lucy came out of the bedroom, dressed, but without the cape. "Thank you, Martha," Lucy said. She turned sad eyes on Jimmy. "And thank you. Staying here helped."

Jimmy nodded and sat down at the small dining table. Lucy helped Martha for a few minutes, and then sat down herself, across from Jimmy.

Martha served them fresh scrambled eggs, toast, hash browns, and reconstituted orange drink. There was homemade strawberry preserves and coffee. Jimmy declined the coffee and said, "I'll have a cup of tea in a while. Just the juice and water for breakfast." The two ate silently, while Martha sat nearby and sipped a cup of the coffee.

Jimmy went outside to clear the accumulation of last night's snow from around the motorhome while Lucy and Martha cleaned up after breakfast. Jimmy was just about to go in when Martha and Lucy both came out of the motorhome, dressed for the weather. Lucy glanced at Jimmy, but said nothing and followed Martha up the path to the barn, struggling in the additional snow on the path.

Jimmy thought about Lucy from time to time, wondering about her, but asked no questions. He put in his time in the greenhouses and the barn, but there were more than enough people to keep things running, so he stayed mostly in the motorhome. He began a journal to occupy his time. He went back to his teen years at the commune and began to record the events of history as he knew and remembered them.

It was again June before the last of the snow had soaked into the earth or run off. Even Jimmy was feeling a bit of cabin fever and joined in enthusiastically in the outdoor work of the farm. But when the planting was done, he felt the wanderlust again and began preparing the Suburban and trailer for travel.

It had been almost two years since the attack and he wanted to recover the caches from the rental rooms in the city, as well as begin his pickup of the rent, assuming some of those occupying them were still occupying them.

From Amateur Radio Broadcasts they'd heard during the winter, the US population had shrunk another ten percent during the winter, after having lost seventy-five percent from the direct effects of the war, and another fifteen percent of those left during the first winter. There was now less than twenty percent of the pre-war population still living, mostly in the southern tier of states where the winters weren't quite as bad.

Jimmy also intended to deal with the group at the sixth quadraplex, which had run him off by force of arms.

On the announced day of his departure from the farm, a small group came to the motorhome to see him off in the Suburban. Jimmy found himself looking to see if Lucy was in the group. She wasn't.

The good-byes said, Jimmy headed down the access road of the farm. Just out of sight of the farm someone stepped out into the road from the trees. It was Lucy MacAtee and she was carrying a duffle bag strapped to her back, and a Steyr AUG slung over one shoulder. Around her waist was a pistol belt with full flap holster and various pouches. Suspended from the other shoulder was a musette bag. Jimmy assumed it contained magazines for the AUG.

Jimmy couldn't figure out why she had the duffle bag, on security patrol. And for that matter, they didn't patrol alone, anyway. Curious, he pulled up and stopped, downing the right side window of the Suburban.

"You want me to take you back up to the farm? You're awfully far out to be on your own."

Lucy looked at Jimmy with at least something of a sparkle in her eyes, Jimmy noted. "No. I'm going with you."

It totally floored Jimmy. He didn't know what he had expected to hear, but it sure wasn't that, even with the evidence staring him in the face.

"In no uncertain terms," Jimmy said, finally getting his composure back, "you are not!"

She was opening the front passenger door. Jimmy tried to hit the lock button, but she had the door open. Leaving it opened she stepped down the side of the Suburban, opened the rear passenger door and slung the duffle bag off her shoulder and put it in the passenger seat. Jimmy couldn't seem to move as she closed the second passenger door, climbed into the front passenger seat, closing the door after her.

"No. You are not going with me. I'm taking you back to the farm as soon as I can turn around."

Jimmy was staring at her and saw the tears form in her eyes. "Please," she said softly, seeming to shrink into herself. "I have to get away from there. At least for a while. There are too many bad memories for me there, right now."

"But…" Jimmy said, and then tried to think of something else to say. Finally, he added, "You can't just take off. You have responsibilities."

Lucy barked a short laugh. "The women are fawning all over me, trying to get me to forget about the baby. That's what I want to do, but they just keep reminding me with their well wishes."

And then, again, came something out of Lucy's mouth that Jimmy was in no way expecting. "My husband said I am very compliant, and very good in bed. You can sleep with me any time you want to, on the trip. The doctor said not to get pregnant, but I have protection. Internal protection." She was looking at Jimmy, eyes open, vulnerable, tears slowly rolling down her cheeks.

"Lucy, no!" Jimmy groaned. "You don't mean that!"

A determined look came over her face. "I do mean it. I'm not saying you have to, if you don't find me attractive, but the option is available whenever you want to exercise it, if you let me go with you."

"Lucy, I…" Jimmy simply didn't know what to say. He didn't want to tell her she wasn't attractive, for she was. But he didn't want to get into the kind of relationship she was offering.

"I'm also a good cook, and better than average shot. And I'm a light sleeper. And an early riser. And…"

"Stop, Lucy, stop. I know you must have very admirable traits for traveling. It's just I'm a solo operation. I'd drive you crazy."

"I'm already crazy," she said, her voice falling, her head going down. "Crazy from grief. Crazy from guilt that it was my fault. Crazy from fear that it will happen again. Crazy… Just Crazy." She fell silent.

Instinctively Jimmy knew what he said next could very well destroy the woman's will completely. "Okay," he said after long moments of thought, "You can go with me and we'll just play it by ear."

Jimmy put the Suburban back in gear and continued down the road without looking at Lucy. He could tell she was wiping her eyes, and straightening up. He heard her blow her nose. Then she turned in the seat slightly and set the AUG beside her duffle bag.

After a few minutes Jimmy looked over at Lucy. "Any time you want to go back, I'll take you. Things can be rough out in the world. Are you sure you have everything you need? You know. Women's things?"

Lucy smiled slightly. "Yes. I have what I need. Unless we stay a lot longer than you usually stay out."

"I doubt we will." Boy, did he doubt it. The very first excuse and Lucy was back at the farm. "Uh… you brought a sleeping bag, didn't you?"

"I brought a sleeping bag," Lucy replied.

"Tent?"

"No. No tent. I heard yours was a big one."

"Oh. Well… Big for one." Jimmy fell silent, and began to concentrate on his driving. The severe winters and lack of maintenance was beginning to show up in deteriorating roads, even the Interstates.

Lucy was companionably silent, lost in her own thoughts.

Jimmy pulled into the forest at the same spot he'd used on his earlier trips.

"We're stopping already?" Lucy asked. It was still some time before dark.

"I usually eat early, and then go somewhere else to spend the night."

"Oh. Okay. It's safer that way?"

"Yeah," Jimmy replied, pulling around the head the Suburban back the way he'd come in.

They got out of the Suburban, carrying their long arms. At her insistence, Jimmy let her fix supper for the two of them, using his camping gear. He showed her where everything was and let her do as she wanted while he cut wood for a fire. Using a fire ring already there, Jimmy built a small fire.

She was efficient as he was. Jimmy had to give her that. She had their simple supper ready in no time. There was also already there a long log suitable as a seat. They sat side by side to eat. Lucy had brought her own eating utensils, though nothing with which to cook, knowing Jimmy would have cooking utensils.

After the meal, and while Jimmy was putting the few things away, Lucy asked, "Do you have a small shovel? I need to go to the bathroom."

Wordlessly, Jimmy pulled Cold Steel entrenching tool from the trailer and handed it to her. Lucy went to the Suburban and got into her duffle bag again, and headed for the edge of the forest, toilet paper in her jacket pocket, AUG in one hand and the shovel in the other.

Jimmy took the shovel from her when she returned and went into the forest himself. Lucy was in the passenger seat of the Suburban when he got back and put away the shovel. When he got into the

Suburban he told Lucy, "There is a good spot to overnight about twenty minutes from here."

Lucy nodded, but said nothing. It was twilight when Jimmy stopped the Suburban in the forest off the road again. Following his quiet instructions, Lucy helped set up the Mountain Hardwear *Trango 3.1* tent. He set a Brunton *Glorb AA* tent light inside and turned it on. While he got his Kifaru *EMR* pack from the back of the Suburban, Lucy got her duffel bag.

Jimmy let Lucy lay out her thin mattress pad and sleeping bag first in the tent and then laid out his own *Therm-a-rest* pad and *Slumberjack* sleeping bag, on the other side of the tent. Without thinking about it, Jimmy began to take off his boots as Lucy re-entered the tent. She too began to remove her light hiking boots.

Suddenly stopping the process of removing his boots, Jimmy cleared his throat and asked, "Uh… How do you sleep? I know a person should sleep in the raw so the clothes don't hold moisture, but… well… how do you sleep?"

"If that is the preferred method," Lucy said, looking over at Jimmy in the soft light, "I'll just sleep in my panties." She had her boots off and reached for the buttons of her shirt.

Quickly Jimmy made his way out of the tent to giver Lucy some privacy. Her voice was soft as it followed him out of the tent. "You don't have to, you know. My offer still goes."

Jimmy didn't reply. He simply stood with his back to the tent until Lucy called to him that she was in the sleeping bag. He crawled back into the tent, turned off the lamp and undressed. When he was in the sleeping bag he said, "There's a pair of moccasins and a flashlight by my pack. You can use them in the night if you need to get up."

"Thank you," Lucy replied.

It was full dark now, and Jimmy's eyes weren't totally adjusted to the blackness. He didn't see or hear Lucy's silent crying as she fell asleep. Jimmy fell asleep wondering how he'd got himself in such a mess.

It was summertime, but the nights were still cold. When Jimmy woke up the next morning he brought his clothes into the sleeping bag to warm them and then quietly dressed, leaving the lamp off. The sky was showing just a little light when Jimmy crawled out of the tent with his PTR-91.

Jimmy quickly turned around when Lucy left the tent a few moments later, wearing her shirt, but with bare legs. He saw enough to know she was wearing his moccasins and carrying the flashlight as she went to the very edge of the woods. He was pretty sure she was carrying her pistol, too. "At least she is keeping security in mind," Jimmy thought.

"I'll be ready in a few minutes," she called softly to him as she returned to the tent. Indeed she was, Jimmy realized, when Lucy came out of the tent dragging her duffle bag, AUG, and musette bag in just a matter of a few minutes.

"I'll start the Suburban to let it warm up while we take down the tent," Jimmy said. He leaned his rifle against the bumper of the trailer and went to roll up his sleeping bag and pad and put them in the pack. With the duffle bag and pack stowed in the back of the Suburban, the two quickly had the tent down and stowed as well.

Jimmy pulled out of the forest onto the road just as the sun fully cleared the horizon. It was an easy routine that day and the next, with a breakfast stop on the road somewhere with a good view, a quick bathroom stop and lunch of jerky or pemmican with a handful of gorp near noon, and an early stop for supper, with a dry camp for the night.

CHAPTER THREE

They began to see a few people the fourth day, as they entered the suburbs of the city. All appeared armed and very cautious, but most would stop and speak to Jimmy and Lucy if Jimmy stopped the Suburban. They found out the city center was still hot, but the radiation was down around the edges.

Jimmy verified the radiation reading with his own meter as he approached the first storage facility where he had a storage room cache. Suddenly he braked hard, and pulled over on the shoulder of the road automatically as he stopped.

He looked over at Lucy, a chagrinned look on his face. "The radiation… It's not high, but it is above background… Your baby…"

A stony look met Jimmy's chagrinned look. "I'm not going to have any more babies. A little more radiation isn't going to make any difference. Except possibly when I die. A year or two difference doesn't matter to me now."

Rather reluctantly Jimmy pulled back onto the road and continued on his way toward the storage facility. He was very disappointed when they entered through the open gate and saw that almost all of the storage unit doors were open. Jimmy drove around to his unit. It too had the door open.

They both got out of the Suburban, as usual, with their long arms in their hands. Lucy saw Jimmy begin to smile when he stepped in front of the door. "Man, they sure trashed it," Lucy said.

"No, actually, they didn't. That's just a whole bunch of junk I use to camouflage the cache. I bet they saw it and decided there wasn't anything of worth here." He began to set things out of the way, making a straight path down the center of the junk while Lucy kept a watch with her AUG at the ready.

When Jimmy was nearly at the back of the room, down the narrow path he had cleared, he said, "Yep. It's intact." He began carrying box after box of #10 canned LTS food from the cache to the trailer. He moved a year's supply of food for one from the cache. Then he pulled out a long wooden trunk with wheels. "Weapons and accessories," he said. Lucy helped him put it into the trailer.

Jimmy recovered ten ammunition cans and added them to the trailer, two at a time. He was breathing heavily by the time he put the last two ammo cans on the tailgate of the trailer.

"Why don't you let me get a few things while you rest," Lucy said.

"Just one more item," he said, going back into the storage room. He returned with a leather teardrop good-posture shoulder bag. The way he was carrying it, Lucy decided, it was very heavy. She confirmed it when he handed it to her and asked her to put it in the front of the Suburban.

He put everything back into the storage room, just the way they'd found it and then they left, leaving the door open.

The second stop went about like the first, except the storage room was still secure. There were people around, but they caused no problems and Jimmy quickly moved the junk, loaded the cached items, and put the rest back, closing and locking the door.

With Lucy along, Jimmy changed his plans slightly. Instead of hitting all four of the remaining storage rooms on the one trip, he decided to only do two of them, and get back out of the higher radiation zone. He'd not told her exactly what his plans were, and she hadn't asked, so she didn't know about the change.

Instead of the rest of the storage rooms, Jimmy headed for the second of the quadraplexes. The second quadraplex, that had been empty during his first trip, was now fully occupied. He didn't actually count, but there seemed to be at least thirty people there, of all ages. It was the first time he was asked for proof of ownership when he said the building was his. The elders of the clan, as Jimmy thought of them, got together for a while, then sat down to talk with him at one of the kitchen tables, amidst half a dozen small children on the immaculate floor.

Jimmy shook hands all around, complemented them on how well they had taken care of the place, and knocked a month off the rent. Then he showed them the basement entrance. Not a single one them had even considered that the quadraplex had a basement. The young men of the group eagerly helped move the cache items to the trailer, paying as much attention to

Lucy as they did to what they were moving. They headed for the third quadraplex.

Again he was run off from his own property at gunpoint. "Vacate or else," he said, and then went back to the Suburban, where Lucy was waiting with her AUG ready.

Lucy saw the glint in his eye and knew Jimmy was not just going to drive away and leave it. She thought about the situation while Jimmy drove off a ways, and found a place to park the Suburban.

Lucy was prepared to argue with Jimmy about helping him get possession of the quadraplex, but he surprised her. "I need you," he said, turning to look at her, "to guard the Suburban. I'm going to go make a statement. Normally I'd park further away and take a couple of days to sneak up on them, but with you here, I don't have to do that. If I don't show up in six hours, I'll be dead, so get in the Suburban and go back to the farm."

He started to get out of the Suburban, but stopped and turned around to the rear seats. He grabbed the leather shoulder bag and dragged it up front. "Here. I want you to take this and keep on your person at all times. Gold and silver are making a comeback and if you run into trouble you may be able to buy your way out if you can't shoot your way out."

He took out several small leather pouches from the bigger bag and handed them to Lucy. He got out of the Suburban before she could react, opened the rear passenger door and put the shoulder bag back inside on the seat.

Lucy got out of the Suburban, AUG in hand and watched silently as Jimmy opened the rear of the Suburban. He took out a long case and opened it. It contained the Barrett sniper rifle. He assembled it, added the scope and the suppressor, and hoisted it up on his shoulder. He motioned to the shoulder bag next to the case. Lucy picked it up and helped him get it on his other shoulder.

"See you in a while," he said and started walking away. Lucy was tempted to follow him, but wasn't sure she would be able to do so. And not at all sure she wanted to see what he was going to do. She'd heard the others at the farm talk about how capable he was and the fact that he was a hard man. No, she decided, she'd stay at the Suburban and do as he'd asked.

Lucy found a good place to sit and watch the area, unseen. She had slipped the leather pouches in her pants pockets and took them out to look inside. From the little Jimmy had said, she assumed it was gold and silver.

It was. Two bags contained twenty one-ounce Gold Eagles each. Another bag had twenty 1/10th ounce Gold Eagles, two plastic rolls of silver dimes, and two plastic rolls of silver quarters. She checked the other two bags. One more bag of one-ounce Eagles and another of mixed gold and silver.

With a quick look over her shoulder, Lucy stashed the bags in individual pockets of her clothing. And then she sat and waited. Lunchtime came and went. She didn't bother to eat. She just waited, keeping her mind blank, but alert.

It was nearing the six hour time limit and Lucy was trying to decide if she should try to follow Jimmy's path through the woods, or just drive up to the quadraplex shooting. But the soft sound of her name coming from behind her startled her out of the reverie. "It's me. Jimmy."

Lucy spun around, half raising the AUG, but it was Jimmy. She kept her voice calm, but said, "A little more notice, next time." Jimmy grinned and nodded.

He put the Barrett and the musette bag back in the rear of the Suburban, the rifle still assembled. Jimmy was more than a little surprised that Lucy didn't immediately start asking him questions, but she held her peace, waiting for him to speak about what had happened if he wanted to open up to her.

She decided he wasn't going to do so as he drove away. They found another place to fix their supper, and yet another to spend the night. It was an easy routine now, Lucy handling the kitchen chores and Jimmy the camp chores.

Only when they were in their sleeping bags, the tent lantern out, did Jimmy bring up what he had done that day. "I left them an unmistakable message. I'll do the same tomorrow and the day after, until they are all gone or dead."

"I understand," Lucy said, wondering a little what Jimmy would do if there had been children involved. There were at least three women she'd seen, but all three had guns in their hands, just as their male companions.

The next morning Jimmy took them some distance away, on an angle, and then left again with the Barrett, the Suburban in a good hiding place, and Lucy in a better one. He was only gone four hours. They moved the Suburban, ate, and waited for near nightfall to move again and set up camp.

"I think tomorrow will do it," Jimmy said that night.

It was much the same the third day. On the fourth day Jimmy was only gone three hours. He looked rather jaunty carrying the Barrett barrel forward over his shoulder as he stepped out of the trees, Lucy thought.

"They are gone. Lock, stock and barrel."

Lucy smiled at his words. When they got to the quadraplex in the Suburban, Lucy decided Jimmy must have cleaned up some things, because there were no bodies about, though there were bloodstains here and there.

Without really thinking about it, Jimmy showed Lucy how to get into the basement, and where the cache was. "We'll load up tomorrow," he said.

Again Jimmy's plans changed, for the following morning a small group of people came walking up to the quadraplex while he and Lucy were having breakfast. There were two women with five men. He and Lucy took up defensive positions, Jimmy pointing out specific spots along the walls that were reinforced to withstand small arms fire. Several of the group was armed, but it looked mainly like hunting rifles and shotguns.

"Hello the house!" the apparent leader called out.

"What do you want?" Jimmy yelled back.

"We want to thank you for running off the vermin that were living here. They've been terrorizing the area for weeks. We saw them pull out yesterday evening."

Jimmy looked over at Lucy. "Believable?" She nodded. "Okay. Keep me covered. If I call you anything but Lucy, open fire. Take out the shotguns first." Again Lucy nodded, just peeking through the open window. Jimmy went out to talk to the small group.

Lucy couldn't hear what was said, but Jimmy turned and waved. "It's okay. We're coming in, Lucy."

She relaxed a little, but kept the AUG ready, standing where she could get into one of the bedrooms if things weren't as they seemed. She relaxed more and shook hands when Jimmy introduced her around.

"These are other local residents."

"Yes," said Jacob Brothers, the leader of the group. "We've been trying to persuade them to leave ever since they showed up and ran off the people that were living here."

"I see," said Jimmy. "Those people still around? The squatters?"

"Oh," said Mrs. Brothers, rather reluctantly, "Three of the families were squatters, I suppose you could say. The fourth family was related to one of the others. The original families all disappeared during the war. We don't know where or how."

"Are those squatter families still here?"

There was a mixed reaction. A few of the group nodded, but two shook their heads.

"Some are, some aren't?" Jimmy asked.

"Yes," said Mrs. Brothers. "The Ames and Zwitecks are living in other houses here in town. The Kragers, both families, left the area looking for better pastures. South."

"Well," replied Jimmy, "I'll make the same deal here as I made at my other properties. I expect yearly rent in some useful form, or gold. A tenth ounce of gold, or what it would buy, per month."

"How much was the rent?" asked one of the others. Jimmy couldn't remember his name.

"Eight hundred a month," Jimmy replied. "That would be the value of two hundred dollars a month now."

"Cash is worthless," Lucy said.

Jimmy smiled. "That's why it is in goods or gold.

Another of the men said, "There are houses for the taking. There is no need to pay anyone rent."

"I agree," Jimmy said. "But anyone living on my property pays rent. And, just so you know, I enforce it with a gun. Just like I did with those that were here and refused to leave when I offered them the chance."

"You're a tough guy, aren't you?" asked the same man.

"So it is said, by some."

The other woman spoke then. "My family would like two of the units. My sister and her family are staying with us. It is so crowded and the house is hard to heat. Mrs. Ames said these units have good wood heaters, kitchen stoves, and even wood water heaters."

"That is true," Jimmy replied. "You're free to take a look. Lucy will show you the rest of the house. There's the main heating stove, there." He pointed to the cheery stove, a fire burning in it to break the chill of the morning.

Jimmy stayed near the open front door of the unit, keeping an eye on the surrounding countryside. Just in case. The group was talking excitedly about the quadraplex when they returned to the living room.

"I'm sure all four units will rent," Jacob said. "At your stated price. How do we get hold of you?"

"I'll contact you. If I happen not to show up for ten years running, whoever is renting can keep the accumulated items. I expect the correct amount to be here when I return." Jimmy paused. "Except, I'll accept if the accumulated money is used for community projects, that the community can pay me when I show up. But the community needs to be prepared for that eventuality."

Jimmy ignored the jabbering among the seven people, walking to the open door to take another look around. "Okay," said Jacob, going over to Jimmy. "The town council will keep an eye on things for you. We'll probably use one of the units for town functions."

"As long as I get my rent. Now if you will excuse us, we'll do a more thorough cleaning, since it appears there will be new tenants soon."

The seven traipsed out, leaving Lucy and Jimmy alone in the unit. "You don't have to help," Jimmy said. "But I do want to clean things up a bit. As a cover for cleaning out the stash."

"That's okay," Lucy replied. "I'll help. I like to see a clean house. The animals that were here were just that, animals."

It took them all day to clean the four units of the quadraplex and move the cache. They stayed the night again in the #2 unit, putting down their sleeping bags in front of the fire after Jimmy again disabled the Suburban and set its alarm, as he did every night.

They'd had their breakfast and the Suburban was warmed up the next morning, when Jimmy said, "Hang on a minute. I want to uncover the outside basement entrance."

She followed him around the building to unit #4. Under the living room window he began to dig. Lucy follow suit, having taken up a shovel when Jimmy did. It only took a few minutes to uncover and open the door.

"That was a nice thing you did," Lucy said, "Letting them have the basement, too. Like the others."

"Bah! Humbug!" Jimmy said, half under his breath. Lucy just smiled.

Jimmy was cautious when he pulled up to the fifth quadraplex. The tenants had been pleasant enough when he stopped in on his first trip. He wasn't counting on the same greeting. But there were children playing in the yard. "Just the pistols," Jimmy said. He looked over at her. Lucy was looking at the children. "Don't get distracted," he said, as kindly as he knew how.

Lucy started guiltily, but nodded. They both got out of the Suburban and were immediately mobbed by the children asking questions. Who they were, where did they come from, could they have a ride?

Jimmy led the way, wading through the children, until he got to the front door of Unit #1 of the quadraplex. He knocked on the door.

A totally amazed, buxom woman, in a skin tight blouse answered. "Hi. I'm Jimmy Holden. I'm here to collect the rent."

"George!" roared the woman over her shoulder. A big man, one of the ones Jimmy had talked to on his earlier trip, came running from the kitchen.

"Oh," he said, sliding to a stop. "It's you. The rent guy." Jimmy nodded.

"All we gots extry is fire wood. You didn't want it before."

Lucy suddenly touched Jimmy's shoulder and jerked her head. Approaching from around the corner was a very dapper looking man for the times, dressed in black, carrying a black walking stick, with a single action revolver in a black holster on a black gun belt.

"I'm the law here," he said. "What is the problem? I heard Mrs. Haverton call out."

"I'm Jimmy Holden. Here to collect the rent."

"Let's see the proof." Jimmy handed it to the man in black.

"It's real, George. Pay up. That firewood you've been saving up since I've known you." The man in black handed Jimmy back the documentation. "I'm in #2," he said. "Come around when you're done here and I'll give you my share."

Jimmy nodded and turned back to George. "Still don't need the firewood, but someone will. I'll find a trade for the wood and come back." He wasn't asking. He was telling.

Jimmy and Lucy went to the door of #2 and knocked. The man in black opened it. "I'm Sheriff Anthony Jones. I was told gold and/or silver was acceptable." He pulled a leather coin case from a pocket of his black leather vest. "A tenth ounce of gold per month or equivalent."

Jimmy nodded and the man took a one-ounce gold Krugerrand from the coin case. "I assume you can make change. I've been here seven months." He was looking Jimmy straight in the eye.

Jimmy's small smile curved his lips. "Sure. Unless you want some firewood."

The Sheriff looked startled.

"I plan to trade off the firewood. I can't take it all with me. I'm giving you first chance at it, at a discounted rate. I like having the law living in my place."

"Yes. One does. How much?"

"Let's see how much there is."

They walked around the quadraplex to where the wood was neatly stacked and covered with old tarps. "Looks to be fourteen cords," Jimmy said. "A cord a month for the rent. Makes it a tenth-ounce per cord. Twenty-one tenths for the seven months' rent and fourteen cords of wood. Make it easy and call it two-ounces even."

Lucy could tell that the Sheriff was reluctant, but he gave Jimmy another Krugerrand. "Thank you," Jimmy said his smile larger now, and not quite the same.

He and Lucy went back to the quadraplex and knocked on the door to #3. George had come out and stood out of the way while Jimmy and the Sheriff were looking at the firewood. "I think the Tanenbaughm's are both working. In town, at the old hotel."

"Thanks," Jimmy called. "By the way, I made a deal for the firewood. You're paid up." He went over to the door of #4 and knocked. It was opened by a woman with a very large revolver pointing at Jimmy.

Jimmy didn't flinch, though Lucy stepped back. "Just here to collect the rent," Jimmy said. "I don't remember you from my last trip."

"I'm new. Only been here a few months. They said someone would be here for the rent. I didn't believe them."

"Should have," Jimmy said his voice even. "You can pay, or you can leave."

The woman hefted the revolver. "This says I won't."

"No it doesn't," Jimmy said, snatching the gun from the woman's hand before she could react. He handed it back to Lucy. "Look," he continued. "I'm not unreasonable. Anything of value is acceptable."

The woman leaned out of the door and looked at Lucy, and then back at Jimmy. "If you didn't already have a woman, I'd let you take it out in trade."

Before Jimmy could say anything, Lucy spoke up. "We aren't together like that. He can have you if he wants to. I'll wait in the truck."

"I do not want to take it out in a trade like that!" Jimmy said forcefully. "Anything of value will do. Except that."

"Your loss," said the woman. "I'm very good. I don't like to spend my gold and silver. How much that way?"

"Tenth-ounce of gold per month. How long have you been here?"

"Seven months," she replied. Neither Lucy nor Jimmy commented on the fact she'd been there the same amount of time as the Sheriff.

"Seven-tenths an ounce total," Jimmy said.

"I guess it is easiest. And I can get more." She glared at Jimmy. "Expect chickens and a pig next year."

"That will be fine," Jimmy said.

The woman reached into her cleavage and pulled out a silk bag. She counted out the seven-tenths of an ounce, giving Jimmy a very warm half-ounce Eagle, and two equally warm tenths.

"Thank you," Jimmy said. Lucy handed him the revolver and Jimmy handed it to the woman. "I'll see you some time next year."

She closed the door in his face.

"Let's go find the Tanenbaughm's," Jimmy said, turning to Lucy.

SCAVENGER

Lucy found herself smiling as she looked out the passenger window as Jimmy drove them toward the town's downtown district. The hotel was easy to find. It looked like it was the center of action, post war. There were three vehicles and half a dozen horses near the entrance. Jimmy parked and he and Lucy went in.

"We're looking for the Tanenbaughm's," Jimmy told the first person they saw. The woman was at one of several desks scattered about the lobby. She pointed toward the reception desk. Jimmy and Lucy went over.

"Mr. Tanenbaughm?" Jimmy asked the man sitting behind the long counter.

"Yes," the man said, looking up. "Oh. You. You did come back. The wife said you would. I didn't think so. Figured someone would have killed you by now."

"Not yet," Jimmy said. "What do you have for me?"

"It will have to wait until I'm off work. Meet me down at Bronson's at four."

"Bronson's?" asked Jimmy.

"The town butcher."

Jimmy nodded. "We'll find it. Four o'clock."

When they were back in the Suburban, Lucy asked, "Are we going to empty the cache?"

Jimmy shook his head. "I don't think so. I don't completely trust that Sheriff. Think I'll wait on this one." They killed the time checking out the small town. It seemed to be making a real comeback. The government, such as it was, was based at the hotel. There seemed to be activity on many of the streets. People were friendly wherever the pair stopped. Having seen the sign at the butcher shop, Jimmy pulled up and parked right at four.

Lucy went inside with Jimmy after he locked the Suburban. Tanenbaughm came in only moments later. Tanenbaughm went over to the counter and spoke to the clerk. "I'm here for that meat," he said.

"Meat?" Jimmy asked.

"Yes. My brother raises beef and swine. I help him out and he gives me part of his harvest. I've had part of it preserved as my rent."

"Sounds okay to me," Jimmy said.

The butcher went into the back and came back a few moments later carrying a large tote. He set it down on the counter and went back to get four more of the totes.

"Jerky, some hams, bacon, summer sausage. Everything will keep until you get it back home," Tanenbaughm said. "I hope it is enough. I don't really have anything else to give you."

"It'll be fine," Jimmy said. "Hickory smoked?"

The butcher nodded. "Salt cured hams, hickory smoked. The bacon, too. The summer sausage is a standard mix. The jerky is plain. Just a touch of salt."

Jimmy and Lucy carried everything out to the Suburban, with Tanenbaughm's help. They shook hands and then Jimmy and Lucy drove off, headed for the sixth and last quadraplex. On the way, Jimmy explained what had happened on the first trip out.

They took their time getting to the last quadraplex, camping out beside a river a couple of days to replenish their water, and take the opportunity for a quick, rather cold, swim. When they reached the town, Jimmy went directly to the quadraplex. Again he was told to leave and not come back.

Jimmy found a good spot to camp outside of town, and they set up camp. As he had before, Jimmy uncased the Barrett and went hunting. It went much the same as it had at the other hostile holding, except it took four days of sniping before the group cut and ran during the fifth day, as Jimmy watched through the Swarovski scope on the Barrett.

He continued to watch for two more days, carefully scouting the area. Sure enough, he found two snipers waiting, with the rest of the group holed up nearby. He eliminated the snipers, and put two rounds into the group's new temporary home. Jimmy tracked the group when they left, until he was sure they were headed away from town permanently.

It had taken a week, but Jimmy and Lucy had occupancy of the quadraplex. Like the first one they'd liberated, this one was a pig sty. They began to clean it up. Besides the cache they recovered, Jimmy and Lucy loaded up what firewood had been left from the previous winter, and the few useful items the squatters had left behind. During that time, several curious people cautiously approached, to see what all the commotion in the area had been about.

Jimmy explained that it was his property and he'd run off squatters unwilling to pay rent. Though, like the other quadraplexes, this one had to have water brought in, it was set up well for the cold winters and was therefore of prime interest to those with less amiable accommodations.

In no time Jimmy had five new renters, by opening up the basement and renting it out separately, after removing the cache. It was another small town making a comeback. All the new renters were agreeable to the rent Jimmy was asking, particularly since it could be paid in goods. All five families knew one another and were cooperating on several enterprises. They would pay the rent as a group.

One of the enterprises was biodiesel. Jimmy was able to refill the empty fuel tanks on the Suburban and trailer for just two tenth-ounce Eagles, two hams, a side of bacon, and three summer sausages. In addition to the fuel, the exchange netted them some winter left over potatoes, carrots, and onions.

With summer in full swing, refueled, and with plenty of food from the rent payments, trade, and recovered caches, Jimmy asked Lucy if she wanted to go back to the farm.

"Not really," she said. "I know we have to go back before winter, but I'm in no hurry."

"Well," Jimmy replied, "I consider my first quadraplex a lost cause, but I guess I could check it and see if I can clean it up and put it back in use." He explained what had happened and Lucy made a face. "Ew! How do people live like that?"

"It finally got to them, I guess. There was nobody there when I pulled the cache. I'm not really sure it is worth it. I may just pull the wood stoves and let it go at that."

"That sounds like a very good plan," Lucy said with a smile.

They took their time, camping out in wooded areas and going through the towns on the route without stopping until they got to the quadraplex. Wildlife was making a strong come back in the area, despite the heavy hunting and since they weren't actively hunting, Jimmy and Lucy often got close looks at the wildlife.

Then they were at the quadraplex. And much to their surprise, especially Jimmy's, all four units were occupied. They got out of the Suburban and Jimmy introduced himself. Like another of the quadraplexes, this one was tenanted by an extended family clan.

"I'm Joe Gladstone," said the senior member of those that came out of the building to greet Jimmy and Lucy. Weapons were around, Jimmy noted, but there were no threatening moves of any kind.

Jimmy heard a generator running. It looked like all of the yard space of three of the units was garden. The fourth yard had obviously been disturbed, but had grass growing on it.

"How did you decide to move in?" Jimmy asked. "When I checked a little over a year ago, there was a foot and a half of sewage in the basement, and the pipes were all busted up."

Joe replied, "I'm a plumber. Wasn't that much trouble to pull the floor drain grate and flush the basement out, and scrub it down with swimming pool chlorine. Fixed the plumbing, put in a septic system, well and generator. With the wood stoves in the units, and the way they are built, it was no real problem. You aren't going to try to make us move out, are you?"

Jimmy shook his head. "I've been collecting rent on my other properties, had essentially abandoned this one. Since you've done so much to recover and put it back into use, I'll just have to give the deed to you."

Joe's eyes lit up. "Really?"

Jimmy nodded. He went back to the Suburban, opened up his briefcase and took out the deed. He signed it over to Joe and gave it to him as Lucy looked on.

"Well, consider yourselves always welcome at our door," Joe said, taking the deed gingerly.

"Since you mention it, and you have running hot water, and we've been camping out the last several weeks, I wonder if we might use one of the showers?"

"Why, certainly!" Joe boomed. "Annabelle, show these nice folks to our bathroom."

"Come along, honey," Annabelle said, leading Lucy toward the building. "Ladies first."

"Let me get my bag," Lucy said eagerly. She went to the Suburban and then followed Annabelle.

Joe and Jimmy sat down at Joe's kitchen table and discussed the surrounding area while Lucy was getting her shower.

It was near noontime, and Joe and Annabelle invited Jimmy and Lucy to stay for lunch. Jimmy suspected it was a bit more elaborate than the family usually had for lunch. Jimmy and Lucy got back on the road shortly after they had their lunch.

Jimmy headed back to the farm. Again they took their time. Jimmy only wanted to get back in time to help with the harvesting. Lucy was in no hurry to get back at all. She and Jimmy had fallen into a companionable relationship. She maintained her modesty and Jimmy made no attempts to take her up on the offer she'd made when she first joined him on the journey.

On the last night before they would be back at the farm, Jimmy cleared his throat while they were setting up the tent for the night. "Lucy. Um… Well… I want to say you've been far more help on this journey than hindrance. I want you to keep a portion of what I collected in rent… some of the meat. And that gold and silver I gave you that time."

"I forgot all about that," Lucy replied. "It just been automatic to stash it in my clothing when I get dressed, the way you wanted. I'll give it back."

"I didn't bring it up to get it back. I want you to keep it for helping me out. That and your choice of some of the meat."

"I didn't go with you to get paid. I just wanted to get away. I should thank you and… I should thank you, and I do. Thank you."

"Lucy, come on. If you'd been here, you'd have been helping. I don't know what you do to help make ends meet, but you didn't have that opportunity this summer. You need personal funds."

"I can't accept… Well, maybe the meat. My in-laws will certainly appreciate it, but the gold and silver…"

"You earned it," Jimmy insisted.

"Promise me you'll let me go next summer. But no extra money. What you've given me is more than enough."

"Oh. I don't know…"

"Come on, Jimmy. You said I was of help. And we did okay together, didn't we?"

"Well… Yeah. Well, I'm not going to promise, but I will consider it. There are too many variables to say right now."

"Good enough," Lucy said. "I'll keep the gold and silver and take a little of the meat."

It wasn't without some disappointment on both their parts when Jimmy and Lucy parted ways upon their return to the Farm. Lucy went back to her room in one of the Farm houses, and Jimmy went back to his motorhome. He began to help with the harvest, and Lucy began helping with putting it by for the winter.

Things were going quite well when the brothers and sister came to Jimmy's motorhome to talk to him.

"Jimmy," Sheila said, "We have something of a problem. You know we stocked up on replacement grow lights for the greenhouses, like you suggested. Well… It turns out they shipped us the wrong ones. Everything was right on the paperwork. It was just the wrong boxes when he started to get them out. We need to start replacing some or lose a lot of production this winter."

"I see," Jimmy said slowly. "This is bad. No way to convert the fixtures?"

"We could, if we had the parts," said the oldest brother, Frank. "We actually thought about getting parts so we could switch types, if we ran across some, after the fact, but we never did. We need either the parts to switch, or the original style of bulb."

Jimmy nodded. "You want me to go looking."

It was the younger brother, Andrew, who answered. "If you would. It's coming up on winter and I don't think anyone else could handle it. You're used to the travel."

"Of course I'll go. Any clues as to where I might find one or the other?"

"We got the ones we have from a supplier in the city. We're hoping there will still be some bulbs there. We just don't know if the place survived the attack."

"Only one way to find out," Jimmy said. "That's to go and look. I'll head out day after tomorrow."

"Thank you," Sheila said. "We hated to bring this to you. It was our mistake."

"You're right to come to me. I'm much more expendable than any of you. Not to mention more capable at this kind of thing. Don't worry. I'll come up with something."

"I don't know if you can find someone to go with you," Andrew said. "With families to care for and winter coming on…"

"Don't worry about it," Jimmy replied. "I'm used to working on my own."

Jimmy began to get things ready the next morning, servicing the Suburban and the trailer, cleaning his weapons and loading up magazines with rounds. He also went through his winter clothing, his thoughts suddenly going to Lucy. He hadn't seen her for several days.

"No," he thought, "We may have to go through some heavy residual radiation."

But Lucy more or less took the decision out of his hands. She showed up mid-morning, while Jimmy was preparing. "So. I hear we're going grow light hunting."

Jimmy felt his spirits lift. He decided not to fight it. "I guess so. You'll need cold weather gear."

Lucy nodded.

"What else. Your weapons, of course. And…" Jimmy colored slightly.

Lucy noticed and smiled and said, "I have the female things I need."

"A urine diverter?"

"What's that?" Lucy asked.

"A device so women can urinate without having to disrobe so much. Maybe you can borrow one from one of the other women."

"Like any of them are likely to have one," replied Lucy. She looked at Jimmy for a long minute. "You're prepared for most things. I bet you have one I can use.

It sounds like a very good idea. I don't relish dropping my pants every time I need to go to the bathroom."

"Actually," Jimmy said, "I do have a couple." He went to get one of the bags in the second bedroom of the motorhome and carried one back to the living room area. "There're several things you might need that are suitable for winter camping for women. And you can use this pack. It'll be better than your duffle bag. It's like mine, as you can see, but smaller. It's a Kifaru Navigator with the extended top."

"Okay," Lucy said. "I'll just take you up on this. If we can find it, I'll replace everything I use."

"Doubtful, but we might as well scavenge everything we can after we find what we need for the farm. And it won't be quite so bad going to the bathroom. We'll be carrying a chemical toilet. I just don't normally use it for urination."

"I'll manage," Lucy said. "I did before." She paused for a long time. "Jimmy, I'm not going to have children, as I told you before. But what about you? Are you sure you want to do this. We could get a pretty good dose of radiation, depending on circumstances."

"I think you should reconsider your options, Lucy. I'm not worried about myself. I am about you."

"Don't be. I've made up my mind," she replied. Jimmy let it drop. Lucy helped him the rest of the day, getting things ready, and he gave her a bit more advice on her own preps for the trip.

CHAPTER FOUR

It started to snow as they pulled away from the Farm the next morning. Jimmy made steady progress, taking the most direct route. At least where the road was good. More than once they had to leave the road to go around blockages from the time of the war, and bad sections of the road due to the weather the past two winters.

As they had the last trip, supper was prepared at one site, and the night was spent at another, more secure site for security reasons. In the pack that Jimmy had given Lucy were two sets of silk long johns that fit her well enough to wear on the trip. It was what she slept in. And since she was covered, Lucy didn't bother to wait for, or ask Jimmy to leave the tent when she undressed down to the silks and crawled into her sleeping bag.

Jimmy knew Lucy had no idea how provocative the sight of her in the silk long johns was to him. He said nothing, but made sure he was turned away from her when he stripped down to his own silk underwear.

As soon as they hit the edge of the city on the morning of their third day out, Jimmy began stopping every so often until they found an intact city yellow pages. So far the radiation was under 0.1R/hr and

Jimmy wasn't worried about it. They found a phone book and looked up the physical address of the supplier for the original grow lamps for the greenhouse.

It was in an industrial section of the city, and many of the narrow streets were blocked. Jimmy put Lucy behind the wheel of the Suburban, and handled the cable for the winch. Jimmy would direct Lucy where to stop, and then hook up the winch cable. Using the remote control, Jimmy would pull the vehicle clear enough for the Suburban and trailer to get through.

It was just too awkward to back up the Suburban with the trailer attached to move the vehicles. The hydraulic winch handled the repeated use without problems. They finally made it to the electrical supply house. There were no signs of it having been disturbed since the war. Using the railroad bar from a tool box in the back of the Suburban, Jimmy broke into the building, trying to do as little damage as possible.

Lucy stood guard outside as Jimmy took his Streamlight Litebox ESL from its charger and turned the hand held spotlight on before he went into the building. Jimmy and Lucy both had Motorola FRS/GMRS walkie-talkies. When Jimmy hadn't returned or called her after some time, she keyed her radio and called him.

"Jimmy. Check in."

"Yeah. Things are fine. I'm just having a hard time finding what I'm looking for."

"Okay. Just checking. Be careful."

Jimmy went back to his search. He finally found what he was looking for, made a note of where it was in the large warehouse, and kept looking. He was smiling when he cranked open one of the loading dock doors, startling Lucy.

She whirled around, the AUG coming up to the ready. She lowered it when she saw Jimmy standing in the opening. "Found the mother lode," he said, jumping down. "Replacement bulbs and change out parts for the style they all ready have. Pull the trailer over here and we'll start loading."

Lucy moved the Suburban and she stood by the lift gate of the trailer. Jimmy began to carry box after box out to her to load into the trailer. She was exhausted by the time Jimmy said the box she had was the last one. "Of this stuff. I want to get some solar panels and controllers, too." Lucy groaned.

But she had a chance to rest as Jimmy brought the panels over and stacked them in the doorway. He wanted to help her load them, as they would be a bit awkward for her to handle alone. Finally Jimmy quit moving panels and moved some smaller boxes to the door.

Both the trailer and the back of the Suburban were nearly full when they finished loading. "There are more left. We'll come back and get them on another trip," Jimmy said. He climbed back up onto the loading dock and closed the overhead door. He wedged the man door closed as well as he could and got into the Suburban next to Lucy.

"Tough day," he said. "But rewarding."

"Definitely tough," Lucy said, rolling her shoulders.

Jimmy took them to the edge of the city and stopped at a mall they'd seen on the way in. The snow was really coming down. "Want to do a little shopping?" Jimmy asked with a smile.

"I doubt anything is left. Look at the windows and doors. Everything is busted out."

"Well, if you'll keep an eye on things, I'm going to look around."

Lucy shrugged. "Sure."

Jimmy took his time. Lucy was basically right. There were actually huge amounts of things left, just nothing that Jimmy considered useful. Until he got to the book store. The place had definitely been scavenged, but Jimmy found title after title that he considered useful. He found a cart in another shop and began to load it up with books. He trundled the heavily loaded cart to the front entrance.

Lucy saw him and came to help him carry the books to the trailer. "I want to look around a bit more," Jimmy said, headed back inside. He picked up the occasional item, here and there. The jewelry stores had been virtually stripped, as had the small coin shop in the mall. But Sears still had quite a few hand tools left. He loaded up the cart again and went back outside.

"No diamonds and gold?" Lucy asked him with a laugh as he stacked the filled tool boxes into the trailer.

Jimmy smiled back. "Haven't checked the upper level, yet."

"You're a pack rat, you know," Lucy said as Jimmy headed back inside the mall. When his head cleared the upper floor level as he climbed the stilled escalator, something caught his eye and he quickly squatted down, bringing the PTR-91 around from its shoulder slung position.

"Lucy," he called on the radio, his voice low, "take up a secure position. I just found expended brass. I'm going to check it out."

"Roger."

Cautiously, Jimmy took the last few steps of the escalator and moved quickly to a heavy planter box where he could get a better look around. There was brass and expended plastic shot shell cases here and there all over the floor. Jimmy began to follow the trail of spent shells. They led him to the only closed business entrance he'd seen in the mall.

The floor was covered with spent shells in front of the metal mesh security grate. Crouched down, Jimmy surveyed the area, both outside and inside the business. A close look showed that the lock near the floor of the security grate had been shot loose. He carefully tried to lift the gate.

He could lift it a foot or two, but no more. It was too heavy. He debated for a few moments and then lifted the gate and rolled under it. Jimmy quickly moved out of sight of the mall walkway, and looked over the store. It was a small specialty shop for sunglasses. Jimmy moved enough to see around behind the sales counter.

What he saw brought him up short. A man and woman lay dead on the floor. Long dead. They looked leathery. Both were in jeans, tee-shirts, and black leather jackets, with Nike running shoes on their feet. Jimmy decided they were probably both in their twenties.

He went over and gathered up the weapons lying beside, on, and under the bodies. There were two Colt 1911 pattern .45 ACP's, a twelve gauge double barrel whippet shotgun, a Bushmaster AR-15 collapsible stock carbine, a Micro-Uzi 9mm pistol, and an old Smith & Wesson Model 59 9mm pistol.

There were several empty magazines laying around for everything except the whippet. The male body had a leather bandoleer of shotgun shells on under the leather jacket. Jimmy checked further and found shoulder holsters on both bodies, the one on the man with an offside suspension system for the whippet.

Both also had on cheap day packs. The jackets were riddled with bullet holes, so he discarded them when he stripped the bodies of the packs and harnesses. He opened one of the back packs and whistled. Jimmy checked the other. It had similar contents.

His theory, from the evidence, was that the pair had robbed the jewelry stores and coin shop and run into armed resistance. They were trying to escape and managed to get into the sunglass store and drop the gate. They held off those trying to either recover or steal from them their booty, but eventually died from their wounds after everyone headed for shelter from the fallout.

Jimmy moved everything he wanted over to the grate, slid under it and pulled the items to him. He found another cart and loaded up, making a quick turn around the rest of the upper floor of the mall, adding items from first one shop, and then another. The upper level just didn't seem to have been as heavily scavenged. He found a second cart and loaded it, too. He stood in front of one shop for several long moments, and then went inside, coming out a few minutes later to add a garment bag to the pile in the second cart.

He headed back to the Suburban, taking his time going down the stopped escalator with the carts.

"I'm coming out," he said on the radio. "Everything is okay."

"Took you long enough," Lucy was saying as he pushed one cart and pulled the other one through the entrance of the mall. "And I can see why," she added when she saw him.

"I'd go take a good look around the upper level. You might find something you can use or get for trading purposes. Don't bother with the sunglass store, I cleaned it out."

Lucy shook her head and started to decline the offer. "Oh, why not," she said.

Jimmy transferred his haul to the Suburban while Lucy went inside. The snow was getting deeper and heavier.

She took a cursory look around, and then wandered the lower level of the mall, despite Jimmy's advice. After a quick look over her shoulder to make sure Jimmy wasn't anywhere around, she went into the shop she had spotted. She came out several minutes later with a pair of large bags in her hands.

Lucy immediately went into a store next door and put the bags from the first store into that store's bags, and then she began looking at more stores. Like Jimmy, she hunted up a couple of carts to carry her finds. Suddenly, while she was on the second level, Lucy noticed that it was getting dark. She hurriedly checked the last couple of shops on the second level and headed back toward the entrance.

Jimmy stopped what he was doing, clearing snow off the Suburban and trailer, and went to help Lucy with her acquisitions. "Seems you changed your mind."

Lucy blushed a little and nodded. "Some things for me, but a lot for some of the people at the Farm. Probably Christmas gifts. Try to pay back some of the kindness people have shown me since I lost Jack, and then the baby."

"I definitely intend to keep some of the stuff I found, but I think I'll just give you the rest to parcel out the way you think best. Other than there at first, we're the only ones that have had the chance to do much scavenging."

"You should give it to whomever you chose, for your own reasons."

"Easier if you do it," Jimmy said, setting the last bag into the Suburban.

"You just don't want to be fussed over by grateful people. Well, I don't either. I say we just give what we aren't keeping to the Farm and let the leadership distribute it."

"No reason for you not to give the stuff you want as presents. You can't go by me. I'm a Scrooge. Bah. Humbug."

Lucy laughed and Jimmy found it a very pleasant sound. "I'll think it over," she said. "Boy," she added, looking around, "It's really been coming down!"

"Yeah. We'd better find a place quick, or we may just have to stop when we can't go any further."

They got into the Suburban and Jimmy turned it toward the Farm. At the first place with some trees, he pulled over. "I don't think we have to worry about a dry night camp. We'll just set up here for the night."

When he got out of the Suburban, Jimmy fished out the Brunton weather instrument and held it up in the freshening breeze. He noted the readings and put it aside to help Lucy set up the tent. They were an experienced team now and the snow did little to slow them down. When Lucy reached for the privacy enclosure Jimmy said, "Hang on a minute." He took out the Brunton weather instrument again and took a look.

"Don't bother," Jimmy said, putting the weather instrument away. "It's going to get bad tonight. We'll just put chemical toilet in the rear vestibule and call it good. Is that okay? I can always step outside when you need to use it."

Lucy shrugged. "It should be okay. I trust you." She looked up at the sky. "This is the first heavy snow of the year. It shouldn't be too bad, should it?"

"I don't know, Lucy. The barometric pressure is dropping, the snow has been getting heavier, and the wind is picking up. We may be here a day or two."

"Oh," was all Lucy said.

They took their back packs into the tent, and the provisions bag and water bladders. Jimmy also brought in the Yaesu FT-817ND Amateur radio, a couple of extra blankets, and a bag that Lucy didn't recognize. They spread one of the blankets out on the floor of the tent for insulation.

Both pulled off their winter boots when they entered the tent for the last time. Jimmy took a pair of shearling moccasins out of his pack and put them on. Lucy put on an extra pair of socks. They were set for the duration.

Though the Farm kept a radio watch around the clock, Jimmy seldom checked in. However, under the circumstances, he had decided he should, to let those at the Farm know he'd found the bulbs and they were settled in for the storm.

Jimmy attached the Miracle Whip tunable portable whip to the Yaesu, punched in one of the frequencies the Farm monitored and filled them in on the situation while Lucy set up the MSR Whisperlight Internationale single burner stove in the front vestibule of the tent and began to heat water to prepare a freeze dried meal, and for hot tea and coffee.

After he'd finished the radio contact, Jimmy checked the weather instrument again. The barometric pressure was still falling. Looking out of the vestibule window of the tent, Lucy said she could barely see the Suburban and there were already several inches of accumulation since they'd stopped. Both could tell the wind had really picked up, the way the tent was shaking occasionally, despite having set up the tent on the downwind side of the Suburban.

"This could turn into a real blizzard," Jimmy said. "Boy, I miss the Weather Channel." As they began to eat they discussed a few of the things they missed with the way civilization was now. They also discussed some of the positives. Though it was still fairly early they turned out the tent lamp and went to bed.

Sometime during the night Jimmy heard Lucy stir and get the second blanket with which to cover her sleeping bag. By his luminescent watch it was a little after 2:00 AM when Lucy stirred again and softly called over to him.

"Jimmy? Jimmy, I'm cold."

"Here," he said, "Scoot your bag and mattress over against mine. We can snuggle up and you can share my warmth."

Lucy didn't hesitate. She scooted over as close as she could get, with her back to him. Jimmy pulled the blanket over their sleeping bags, and then reached over, half rolling onto Lucy to pull the floor blanket up and over her.

He worked his arm under the two blankets and put it over Lucy's upper body, pulling her against him. "Thanks, Jimmy. This is much better. I guess my bag isn't good enough for weather like this. I'm sorry."

"Don't worry about it," Jimmy replied. "And we'll be able to warm up the tent in the morning. "I have a few propane cylinders and a Coleman tent-safe heater. It'll be enough to take the chill off before we get up, but I don't want to run it during the night…"

"Okay. Thanks, Jimmy." It was only moments and Lucy's breathing was slow and even. She'd fallen asleep. It took Jimmy a while longer.

When he woke up around five the next morning, he was on his back, and Lucy, sleeping bag and all, was lying half on top of him, her left arm out of her bag, around his chest, under the blankets. She was still sleeping soundly. Jimmy didn't want to wake her so relaxed and let himself fall asleep again.

The wind slightly flapping the tent woke him the next time. Lucy was now facing away from him, her back right up against his side. As soon as he moved slightly, Lucy said, softly, "You awake, Jimmy?"

"Yeah." He checked his watch. It was 7:33 AM. "If you're ready, I'll get the heater going and we can get up and get dressed in a few minutes."

"No arguments from me." She reached over, found her clothes in the faint light and pulled them into the sleeping bag with her with a suppressed squeal when the cold clothing touched her silk layer.

Jimmy climbed half way out of his bag, enough to reach the bag Lucy hadn't recognized the evening before. It clanked slightly. He took out the Coleman heater, inserted a propane bottle and hit the built-in striker. When the heater was going he set it safely away from them and snuggled back into the sleeping bag, bringing his clothes in with him.

It took several minutes to take the worst of the chill off and both Jimmy and Lucy fell asleep as they waited. Another series of wind gusts woke them both. While not toasty, the tent was significantly warmer now and both quickly climbed out of their sleeping bags, used the chemical toilet in turn, and then dressed.

Jimmy slipped on his boots, but didn't tie them. "I'm going out to take a look around."

"Okay," Lucy replied. "I'll get breakfast started."

Jimmy was gone a long time, it seemed to Lucy. The water was hot and she'd added some to the oatmeal packets they were having for breakfast, and had filled their cups with tea for Jimmy and coffee for her. She was reaching for the FRS/GMRS walkie-talkie to call him when he unzipped the fly vestibule and entered the tent, sitting down in the entrance to take his boots off and clean them. He dusted the snow on his pants legs off, and then came into the tent, zipping up the door of the tent when he did. He was carrying the two small backpacks he'd recovered in the mall.

Setting aside the packs and weather instrument he'd taken out with him, Jimmy said, "There's a good three feet of snow on the ground and it's still coming down heavily. And you can hear the wind. Blowing pretty steady at twenty-five miles an hour with gusts to over forty. I dug out the Suburban and trailer, but we aren't leaving any time soon. I left the snow against the tent fly for insulation."

Suddenly they heard a loud crack. Lucy jumped and looked alarmed.

"It's down below zero. The sap in the trees is freezing and cracking limbs and trunks of trees. I heard some, not quite so loud, while I was out."

"Oh. I guess there isn't much chance of anyone being out in this. "Well, anyone else but us." She laughed and handed Jimmy his double serving of oatmeal. She had learned his likes and dislikes traveling with him.

"Wild animals, either," Jimmy replied, taking the steaming bowl from Lucy. "From what the guys were saying this fall, the wild animal population has made a real comeback. Including predators. And where there is game, there will be predators. Even in the towns and cities, I expect. Maybe even more so in the cities. The animals had better shelter there than out in the open countryside, except for those that den up, anyway."

"I wonder what happened to all the animals in zoos and parks," Lucy said, rather absently.

Jimmy quit eating for a moment. "You know, I haven't really thought about that. It could be a problem."

"Problem? How?" Lucy asked after swallowing a bite of her oatmeal.

"If the zoo handlers turned them loose, some of them very well might have survived. That includes predators. I can't feature all that many surviving, especially those whose natural habitat is warmer climates, but animals can be pretty adaptable. I mean, most of them adapt to being in captivity. They aren't as adaptable as humans, but some of them are pretty close."

"It was kind of just an idle thought," Lucy replied. "I never thought of it being a danger."

"Well, I sure would hate to run into a snow tiger without being armed."

"Now you're scaring me."

Jimmy laughed. "Don't be. Almost all the zoos are in cities. The chances really are very slim, even if they are real."

"Oh. Okay. That's a little better. But we were, after all, just in the city. It has a zoo."

"That's true. But I'm not going to worry about it."

"Well, if you're not, I'll try not to, either."

After breakfast, and the cleanup that followed it, Jimmy sat cross legged on his sleeping bag, the small daypacks at hand. "I need your advice, Lucy. You know I suggested you bypass the sunglass store?"

"Yeah. How'd you get in, anyway? The grate was down. I saw all the shells."

Jimmy explained what he'd discovered and his conclusions. He touched the packs. "They were wearing these." He opened one and Lucy whistled loudly.

"Quite a haul!" she said.

"Yeah. I'm still debating on what to do with it all. I'm not too big on jewelry and don't want much of it myself. But like we talked about the other stuff… I'm not sure to give some of it as gifts, or just turn it over to the Farm. There are certain things I'm keeping."

Jimmy showed her the GIA certificates, with a tiny zip-lock bag stapled to each. "These are investment grade diamonds. They may be worth something, someday, for international trading, if it ever makes a comeback."

"You think big!"

"Civilization is continuing, even if in altered form. People's wants, needs, and beliefs will carry on. Gold and silver are already making a comeback. You get a share, for being with me and standing guard while I scavenged. That includes the good diamonds."

"All diamonds are good," Lucy said. "Take it from a woman. You keep the important stuff. You wouldn't happen to have something with real rubies, would you? I'm a Cancer. Ruby is my stone."

"Go through the stuff and take anything you want as your share." Jimmy felt just a little bad about not showing her everything that had been in the packs. He cleaned out everything he really wanted before bringing the packs in.

That had included the bulk of the GIA diamonds, gold and silver coins, and a few jewelry objects that had caught his eye.

Jimmy enjoyed watching Lucy 'shop'. "You know, you aren't limited to just one," he said at one point when she set aside one item for another.

"I don't want to be a hog," she replied.

"Well," Jimmy admitted, "I should tell you I've already made my selections. This is just the stuff I didn't want."

Lucy laughed. "Oh, yeah. Tell me that now, after I've been through most of it." She seemed to be having a good time. "Is it okay if I take a few items to give as presents?"

Jimmy nodded. "Sure. Whatever you want is yours to do with as you wish." He noted Lucy went over the remaining stuff with a different eye, and then went back over what she had already been through once.

"You didn't take all the gold and silver?" she asked, looking up at him.

"I thought you might want some, and I think some should go to the Farm."

"Okay." Lucy took half of the remaining gold and silver coins, leaving the rest. "What do you think?" she asked Jimmy finally, holding up to her neck a simple ruby necklace.

"Nice," Jimmy said. "Very nice. I actually thought of you when I saw that." What he didn't say was that he'd found one even nicer, along with a few other things that had made him think of her.

"I think the rest should go to the Farm to be distributed or held for trading."

"I agree," Jimmy said, closing up the small backpacks.

"What about the other stuff?"

"Too bulky to bring into the tent. We can go through it when we get home."

Lucy nodded. "You want to play cards?"

"Not right now," Jimmy replied. "I want to catch up my journal."

"That's not a bad idea. I think I'll do the same. I've been trying to keep one, after I saw you doing it last trip."

They settled in for the day, and after their journal entries, they began to play two-handed solitaire for something to pass the time. At first there was little discussion, but then they began to talk, first about simple things, then more serious things. They learned quite a bit about one another that day and afternoon, including a teary rendition of how Lucy had lost her husband right after she'd become pregnant.

The blizzard was still raging when darkness fell and they turned on the Brunton GLORB tent lantern. "Lucy, look…" Jimmy said rather hesitatingly as they cleaned up after the evening meal. "I don't want you to think I'm trying to take advantage of the situation, or take you up on that offer last summer, but my double bag sleep system will separate and zip together to make a double wide bag. And yours will open up like a blanket.

"If you are comfortable with it, we can sleep together in mine, and use your bag and the blankets to add warmth." Suddenly Jimmy hesitated, and then added, "Oh. It just occurred to me. If you don't want to, and since I sleep pretty warm, anyway, I can use your bag and you can use mine. You should be warm enough that way. That's probably the better option."

"Better why?" Lucy asked, watching Jimmy's face.

"Well… because we wouldn't have the hassles of sharing a bag."

"What hassles?"

"Look, Lucy, you're an attractive, sexy woman. I can't guarantee what my physical reaction might be if we're in the same bag. I can guarantee that nothing would come of it, but still…"

"I know enough about winter camping to know keeping warm is critical. I'll make sure I have better preparations next time, but for the moment, keeping warm is more important than modesty or propriety. I think we should share the bag. I know I'll sleep warm enough that way and that you will, too."

Jimmy took her at her word and separated his inner and outer bags to zip them together, while Lucy opened hers out into a blanket. They arranged the bags and blanket and adjusted the blanket on the floor so Lucy could pull it up and over her side of the sleeping bag if she needed additional warmth.

Jimmy got undressed down to his silk long johns and slid into the sleeping bag while Lucy was using the chemical toilet. He turned his back to the rest of the tent while Lucy undressed down to her long johns. She slipped into the bag beside him and turned off the GLORB.

"Boy," she said, squirming around to find a comfortable position, "You are a furnace, aren't you?"

Jimmy just mumbled something and turned his mind to everything except Lucy in the bag next to him. Her back up against Jimmy's, Lucy quickly fell asleep. It took Jimmy longer, but he, too, was soon asleep.

The wind died down during the night and the two slept soundly, Lucy rolling over fairly early in the night, to snuggle her body against Jimmy's, her left arm going over his chest, and her head resting on his out-flung arm.

Lucy woke up first the next morning, in the same position. She made no move to move away from Jimmy, or even change position. She just sighed contentedly and fell back asleep. When she woke up again an hour or so later, it was with her cheek on her own arm, lying face down on Jimmy's side of the sleeping bag.

She rolled over and looked around the tent. The heater was going and Jimmy was already dressed. He was making their breakfast in the front fly vestibule. Sliding out of the sleeping bag, Lucy used the chemical toilet for pressing needs, and then hurriedly slipped back into the sleeping bag with her clothes, to warm them up.

Before she was ready to get dressed, Jimmy carried over a plate with scrambled eggs and ham. Lucy sat up cross legged, pulling the free blanket up over and around her shoulders. "I could get used to this breakfast in bed thing," she said with a laugh, taking the plate from Jimmy. "You'd better be careful not to start a trend."

"No big deal," Jimmy said with a smile. "You were sleeping so soundly. Take a look at the tent wall."

Lucy did so, finally realizing that the snow was almost covering the tent fly. It was actually fairly warm in the tent and Lucy let the blanket over her shoulders slip down as she ate. Jimmy handed her a cup of coffee when she'd finished the eggs and ham.

"The snow has stopped and the wind died down. I held up the Brunton past the snow outside of the tent. It's one degree above zero. The sun is shining. I'll dig out the door of the tent and clean up around the Suburban after a while."

Lucy nodded, savoring the coffee. Her supply was dwindling. She'd miss it when it was gone. Like Jimmy and his M & M's in the gorp trail mix they so often used as dessert. He'd mentioned how much he would miss them the day before. Jimmy was right. There were many adjustments to be made as certain items became either luxury items, or disappeared entirely.

When she made a move to get out of the bag and get dressed, Jimmy put down his cup of tea and said, "I'll start clearing the entrance."

As he unzipped the vestibule, Lucy shook her head and looked down at herself. She considered herself very matronly, in the long handles, even if they were silk. But Jimmy was reacting almost as if she was naked, never looking at her when she wasn't fully clothed. A small smile curled her lips. He obviously found her attractive enough to be a bother to his libido. That was something. His reactions to her during their time together had been anything but romantic. Jimmy had seen to that.

Her smile faded. "Don't be thinking such things, girl. You've made your peace with being a childless old maid. Best you stick to it," she thought to herself.

Lucy followed Jimmy out, after she'd dressed and began to help him clear the snow from off the Suburban, and then from around it again. It took some time, Jimmy insisting that a path be made in front of the Suburban, to give them a good start when they left. He fully intended to leave before all the snow was gone, but not until after at least some of it had melted away. He didn't want an ice pool around the rig.

When Lucy asked him about clearing around the tent, Jimmy said, "Not today. Won't be a lot of melt accumulating under it today. Might as well have the insulation until things warm up and the snow really starts to melt."

Both had shed an outer layer, despite the cold, while shoveling the snow. As soon as they stopped, the extra layer went back on. Neither seemed inclined to go back inside the tent after having been cooped up the way they had.

Jimmy decided to open a path to and around the nearest tree, so he could use it instead of the chemical toilet for part of his sanitary needs. Lucy tried it out first, fetching the urine diverter from her pack in the tent. Jimmy moved to the rear of the trailer and kept himself busy while Lucy was around the back side of the tree.

"This thing is great," Lucy said, coming back from the tree. "Still warm and toasty. Thanks, Jimmy."

Jimmy waved his hand and went to take his turn.

With nothing more to do outside, they both went back inside the tent and got comfortable. They played more cards, wrote in their journals, and since they had plenty of light coming through the top of the tent, both broke out paperback books they'd brought with them for just such an occasion.

Both dozed off and had a long nap after their lunch of jerky and gorp. When they went outside to go to the bathroom, Jimmy was amazed to note that the temperature on the Brunton weather instrument was up to fifty-six degrees. The snow was glazing over, but melting from below due to the ground still being relatively warm. They shared the sleeping bag again that night, but the following night, with the temperature the night before having been in the low forties, opted to use their individual bags.

Less than two feet of quickly melting snow was left when they got up that morning. After breakfast they shoveled out the tent and took it down, spreading it out on the Suburban to dry a bit before they packed it away.

Jimmy started up the Suburban and they left the camp site just after they had a bit of jerky and gorp for lunch. Jimmy had the Suburban suspension lifted as high as it would go, so only the running gear was pushing through the soft, wet snow.

Going was slow, for Jimmy wouldn't take the Suburban anywhere on the road they weren't sure was good, relying on their memory for trouble spots. Jimmy let Lucy drive for the most part, getting out of the truck and taking up a long pole to test the way when they weren't sure what was under the snow.

It was back to their normal travel routine. They stopped early for supper and then moved to another good overnight stopping place. The temperature was in the high sixties when they got up the next morning. More of the snow had melted during the previous day, and overnight, with the warmer temperatures.

They made it back to the Farm late that afternoon and unloaded their things at Jimmy's motorhome after Lucy asked to leave her scavenged goods there until she could sort through them and get them to her room in one of the farm houses.

The family and farm manager were pleased with getting not only many replacement bulbs, but the means to use the ones they'd received in mistake. The usage of the solar panels and controllers was put off until the summer, when they could be installed without dealing with the weather. That was excepting the ones that Jimmy claimed.

Jimmy also turned over the remaining jewelry and coins to the council of the farm that ran things on the Farm, except the actual farming, with the recommendation they do some long range scavenging with some long range plans in mind. One of the elders laughed and said, "We don't have to worry about it, with you making these trips and bringing back what you do."

Jimmy's little smile appeared on his face and he said, "You have no idea what I'm keeping for myself on these jaunts." The elders exchanged looks, but made no response to Jimmy's words. They did, however, start planning some scavenging trips for the following summer, after the crops were in, after seeing the things Jimmy and Lucy brought back for the Farm to use.

Lucy took her time sorting through her goods at Jimmy's motorhome, doing some sorting and arranging and taking a few things at a time back to her room. Sometimes Jimmy was there, sometimes not. He'd told her to make herself at home at one point, and she did. More than once she would cook a meal from the fresh foods the Farm produced and leave it for him, seldom staying until he arrived when he did happen to be gone.

He was spending much of his time learning more about the farm and its operation, as well as going out on the hunting parties that were harvesting wild game to add variety to their diet, despite good production from their domesticated animals.

Thanksgiving was another good one. Things had gone well since the last one. Christmas brought a couple of weddings, and a few very surprised individuals who received some of Jimmy's and Lucy's largesse as Christmas presents. The people receiving the factory made items were those that meant much to them during their time at the Farm.

Jimmy privately gave Lucy one of the finer things he'd kept back from the robbers at the mall. It, like an item she'd picked herself at the time, contained rubies. Several of them, large ones, at that.

"I don't know what to say," Lucy said, putting on the necklace, and then the earrings, the bracelet, and finally the ring.

"You said rubies were your stone. And I simply don't have anything to wear that goes with them."

Lucy's delighted laugh sent shivers down Jimmy's back. He was more than a little pleased, and touched, by the beautiful silk men's shirts she'd found at the mall in one of the women's specialty shops that she was sure that Jimmy hadn't bothered with.

"Thank you," he said, holding the shirts in his hands. "These are great!"

Lucy nodded in response, as pleased as Jimmy at her selection.

CHAPTER FIVE

The long winter finally ended, and the, large, very well trained team of farmers quickly got the crops for that year in, without much help from Jimmy. The Farm elders had him planning a summer long scavenging expedition. The first thing they had said to him about it, other than proposing it, was a question.

"Who do you want to be second in command?"

Immediately he said, "Lucy MacAtee. She's experienced and we've worked together before. She knows my security routines and how I like to operate. She works with all the women here and knows their needs and wants."

The small group exchanged looks. "We'll take that into consideration."

Jimmy smiled slightly. It was a done deal or he was out on his own. The council may very well have picked up on that, for two days later they confirmed her as second in command for the trip, and asked for volunteers to go.

They got many more than they needed, including several additional women. It was left to Jimmy and Lucy to sort down the list to useable size. They interviewed most of them and finally narrowed things down to six others, besides themselves, plus six semi truck driver teams that would be bringing things back as they were found, and a tank truck driver that would drive one of the ten-wheel tanker trucks with biodiesel to keep the vehicles fueled.

One of the criteria for selection was age balanced by physical stamina. They would be going into some higher radiation areas for short times and wanted the oldest people they could get, that could adequately do the work. In theory, they were less likely to have problems from the radiation until very late in life than the younger people. Jimmy and Lucy had already made up their minds about their exposures and would be going in, even in the hotter zones.

Everyone would be wearing dosimeters and anyone receiving more than 25R per week would be barred from continuing for a while. That did include Jimmy and Lucy. The convoy set out when they were relatively certain they'd seen the last of the snow for the season. They missed it by a couple of days, for they ran through some snow as they neared the city on the third day.

Jimmy was using the Suburban to move some obstacles that hadn't been a problem in the past for the Suburban and trailer. But it was easier for Lucy to maneuver the Suburban, since they had cargo capacity and fuel provided by the other vehicles, and therefore weren't pulling the trailer.

Their plan was to essentially avoid what had been open to the public retail places. Not only were they the most likely to have been scavenged by locals, none would have a large stock of any particular item on hand. With Lucy navigating from a marked up telephone book, Jimmy took the convoy to the first of several warehouses he wanted to check.

It took them six weeks of looking to find the things those on the Farm wanted. Most they found in warehouses, but they did start to hit the big malls for some of the other things. Pickings were much better in the higher radiation zones closer to the point where the nuclear device had impacted. Any place that had readings that would put a person over their 25R per week limit in one day was bypassed. They had sent a total of eight semi-truck loads back to the Farm when those on the trip let Jimmy and Lucy know they were ready to go back, since everything on the lists had been found, or it had been decided to be a lost cause.

Jimmy didn't object. He and Lucy were free agents, with no real major responsibility. They certainly did help around the Farm, but at their leisure, where they could. All the others were family people, with specific responsibilities at the Farm.

Summer was on its short downward spiral. It wouldn't be all that long before the short fall would be there and gone. Jimmy looked over at Lucy as the others were climbing into the two Dodge crew cab diesel pickups they had been using on the trip. It took only a quick nod for Jimmy to walk over to the pickups and to tell Frank that he and Lucy wouldn't be back to the farm for a while. They were going to continue to scavenge.

Frank had expected as much. He shook hands with Jimmy. "Okay. Thanks for your help with this. We really picked up many needed items. Don't worry about giving the Farm a share of what you and Lucy find on your own. You've already done enough."

"Okay. But we'll make note of anything that the Farm might find useful so it can be picked up later. We should be back in time for the harvest."

Lucy waved and the two Dodges followed the last semi-trailer and the fuel truck. Jimmy had filled the fuel tanks in the Suburban, as well as the Jerry cans on the rear rack. They didn't have as much fuel as they would with the trailer, but Jimmy decided they would have enough for the trip he wanted to make.

"You ready," Jimmy asked Lucy as they both approached the Suburban.

"Ready. What's the plan?"

"I'm going retirement fund hunting. I want to find a rental place and get a trailer, and then hit a couple of places we bypassed on Farm business, and then the section of the city we haven't been through yet. We can work our way through, and then pick up my last two caches. That sound okay?"

Lucy nodded. Anything would have been fine with her. She just wasn't ready to go back to the Farm yet. Jimmy might not have any romantic interest in her, but he was the most fascinating man she knew and she liked spending time with him. As long as he let her, she was going to continue to do so at every opportunity.

It didn't take long to find a U-Haul rental place and hook up to a tandem wheel enclosed trailer. Jimmy took the time to take a couple of extra spare tires from identical trailers, for the tires on the trailer they were taking were badly weather checked from the years of sitting.

One of the things the Farm had not been interested in finding was a liquor distributor. Jimmy headed directly for one near one of the warehouses the members of the Farm had found many useable items.

The doors of the liquor distribution warehouse were all locked. Jimmy used his tools to open one and he and Lucy went inside with flashlights after Jimmy disabled the Suburban and set its alarm.

"I never realized you were a drinker," Lucy said as they shined the lights around the moderate size warehouse. The shelves were full of colorful cases.

"I'm not, really," Jimmy said. "But many people are. Wine and beer are pretty easy to make. I have the basics to make both, as well as what I need to build a still for simple drinking alcohol. But think of the times twenty years from now. Sure, there will be alcohol for the drinkers, but nothing you will be able to call the good stuff, unless the rest of the world is in a lot better shape than I think it is, and trade picks up.

"I'm limiting myself to three types of things. Even though pure grain alcohol isn't that difficult to make, and will be what I eventually will make, it has many uses, including medical ones. So I plan to take all the 190 proof Everclear I can get my hands on. This won't be the only distributor we hit.

"Next is what I said before. The good stuff. Premium alcohols. The best of the best of each type. I'm not going for the average. I want something a man… or woman… will pay a real price for when the time comes. Even in hard times. Something to keep me fed for a while.

"Last are the specialty drinks, like the really good liqueurs and aperitifs. Frangelica, Galliano, and other 'medicinal', root and herb things the good monks of Europe came up with the last few centuries. And basically anything over a hundred dollars a bottle, wholesale."

They went down the shelves together and Jimmy pointed out what he wanted. He took down a case or two here and there, putting them on the floor for retrieval after they'd gone through the whole warehouse.

Some things were under lock and key in one section of the warehouse and Jimmy broke into it. Definitely high dollar stuff, and only a bottle or two of each. Lucy went looking for some empty boxes and boxed up the individual bottles and carried them out to the trailer. Jimmy stacked everything in just so.

After they were done at the first warehouse it was getting late and they went ahead and ate right there, enjoying a fine wine with the Mountain House meal.

The whole group had not run into anyone during the time that they were there, but Jimmy wasn't going to take any chances. People planning mischief might leave a large group alone, but be more than willing to attack only two people, especially if one of them was a woman. A really attractive woman.

They found a place Jimmy figured was secure enough and they stopped for the night. Jimmy was pulling his tent from the back of the Suburban when Lucy touched his arm. "Jimmy? Can I talk to you a minute?"

"Sure. Any time. What is it?"

"I don't want to set up a separate tent every night like we've been doing. I'm not making a pass or anything, but I'd rather share your tent like we did last summer and fall than be in mine alone. I've gone to wearing a tee-shirt and men's boxers to sleep in. That should be okay, shouldn't it?"

"I won't make anything of it," Jimmy said with a shrug. "I can't say you don't affect me, but I can handle it."

Lucy let the last comment slide into a special compartment in her mind for evaluation later. Now was not the time. They set up the camp the way they had when it had been just the two of them before, and were soon in their individual sleeping bags.

A couple of days into the journey, Jimmy found a yard truck that was still attached to a single axle semi-trailer normally used for city deliveries. He managed to get it to start after he found a bottle of PRI-D in the truck yard workshop. Actually, he found quite a bit of the PRI-D, and even some PRI-G. Apparently the trucking company used the PRI products with all their fuel.

Jimmy doped only the diesel he filled up the yard truck and the Suburban with, plus four empty 55-gallon drums with good tops that he loaded into the semi-trailer and tied off, and then filled with repeated trips with one of the 5-gallon jerry cans. The rest of the PRI products went into the trailer for future use.

He began following Lucy, who was driving the Suburban, with the yard truck and trailer. They'd scavenge during the day, based on what they found in the well worn yellow pages phone book during the evening hours after they'd set up camp.

Jimmy insisted that Lucy consider half of what they found as hers, rather than the scant third he had to talk her into earlier, for helping him. She was doing even more, with driving the Suburban.

More delicate things, like the booze, and very high value things, went into the U-Haul trailer. Everything else went into the semi trailer.

They were zigging into the city to check places, and then zagging back out of the high radiation zones to scavenge smaller shops, to keep their radiation levels lower. But they went over the entire unchecked section of the city that wasn't entirely too hot for them.

They ran into a situation similar to the one Jimmy had found in that first mall they'd scavenged. There were skeletal remains of at least five different bodies outside a gun wholesaler's warehouse in one of the hottest spots they went to. The walls of the warehouse were pockmarked with bullet impacts holes. The heavy steel double door was a sieve of bullet holes.

Jimmy broke out his tools and broke into the warehouse, using extreme caution going in when the door was open. He checked for booby traps, and disengaged four tripwires. Lucy turned away from the sight when they ran across the half eaten remains of three men, two women, and three children. From the looks of it, rats had savaged the bodies after they died.

He couldn't be sure, but only the three men and one of the women showed obvious bullet wounds. He hoped the others had been dead when the rats got to them. Jimmy was more or less inured to such violence, but Lucy was having a hard time keeping her lunch down.

From the looks of it, the owners had successfully defended the warehouse, even though they died in the attempt. Everything was intact. It took them two days to get everything loaded, from the cheapest .25 ACP Raven pistol, to fancy shotguns worth thousands of dollars each in the old days. All the ammunition and reloading supplies were also taken.

They hurried the best they could, not wanting to be in the higher radiation area any longer than necessary. As it was, they took the choice items the first day, left the area, and came back the second day for the rest.

With that much exposure in such a short time, they decided to scavenge the outskirts for a few days before they went into another higher radiation area. Jimmy caught Lucy by surprise when that night they were going over the yellow pages and he asked her if she'd found a Macy's or other upscale department store in the area. She nodded, curious, but didn't ask why and he didn't say.

It was out of the high radiation area, and the mall complex had been fairly heavily scavenged, but when Jimmy found the house wares section virtually intact, he let out a whoop and did a little silly dance.

"What? You planning a new home?"

"Actually, yes," Jimmy said. "Sort of. You know why I got some of the alcohol. Well, to go along with it, I decided to see if I could find some fine china and glassware. We just did."

Lucy didn't laugh. Jimmy was serious. "Oh. Okay then. What are you looking for? Anything specific?"

The two began discussing things as if they were planning a home together. Lucy really got into it. Jimmy didn't take just eight place settings or twelve, or even sixteen. He took every piece he could find of five different patterns, including the displays. The same with crystal glasses and stainless, silver, and gold plated flatware and serving wear. Linens, too. They spent a total of six days at that mall and another high end one, gathering things for Jimmy's planned future business endeavor.

Lucy had some doubts about the idea, but she was enjoying the looking and acquiring. "You know, Lucy," Jimmy said one day in the second mall, "You really should do something like I'm doing. You're going to need a way to provide for yourself when you can't do the physical stuff anymore."

"What," Lucy joked, "You don't think I can get by on my good looks alone?"

Jimmy was very serious when he said, "You could. But you won't. You'll want to make it on your own."

"Oh," Lucy said, a bit taken aback at his seriousness. Wanting to keep things light, she responded, "Well, I'll just be your barmaid until they lay me to rest."

"Sure," Jimmy said. "You have a job with me whenever you want."

Lucy didn't show it, but Jimmy's words had cut her deeply. And she couldn't figure out why. She quit thinking about it as they continued carrying things to the U-Haul trailer.

They began seeing the ducks and geese flying south and decided they needed to wrap things up and head for the farm. It had been four weeks rather than the three Jimmy had initially planned for. They'd been able to extend their time by doping the diesel they found here and there in the industrial sections of the city.

They made two last stops, to pick up the Jimmy's last two caches in the city. With both trailers nearly full they headed for the Farm, leaving as an early fall rain began.

It was not a great harvest, and had it not been for Jimmy sharing some of his stores, Christmas that year would have been anything but a joyous holiday. They made it through the winter; another long, cold one; with no major problems. Everyone looked forward to spring, and the time to begin planting again.

The Farm planned to almost double the number of acres under cultivation. They were beginning to get more requests for trades from some of the surrounding areas. That on top of the shortages they'd had that winter, those on the Farm were not going to take any chances of running short.

They didn't have to worry about meat. The herds and flocks were doing well and were expanding, despite the meat heavy diet the Farm had. There were still animals available for trade, which with produce and biodiesel their main trading goods, the Farm was able to acquire the other things they needed. For the most part, anyway.

Jimmy and Lucy had provided the council a list of things they'd found that the Farm might want, after the Farm team had left them the previous summer. Another scavenging expedition was scheduled for as soon as the planting was completed, again to be led by Jimmy and Lucy.

Lucy went to Jimmy's motorhome two days before they were scheduled to leave. "Jimmy, I need to talk to you about something."

He invited her in and made her a pot of coffee, while he had tea. "What is it, Lucy? You sound serious."

"Well," she said, "What you did last summer, and what you suggested got me to thinking about my own old age. I really do need to come up with a way to support myself when I get older. I like being here on the farm, though it is a bit crowded. But I'm not really part of the family anymore, with Robert gone, and no offspring.

"They've not said anything, of course, but their families are growing and they will soon need the space I am taking up."

"One of those problems is easy to remedy," Jimmy said.

Lucy suddenly drew up slightly, waiting for what Jimmy might say. But it wasn't what she wanted to hear, even though she really wasn't expecting it.

"We can get you a motorhome like mine. I'm sure the family won't mind you setting up out here where I am. It won't be a problem to extend the water line, and my septic system is way over engineered. You could hook up to it with no problem."

Lucy nodded. Again, it wasn't what she wanted to hear, but it was what she expected. "I thought about that, but I wanted to get your opinion. I know you like your privacy, but this is the best spot on the Farm, in my opinion and I didn't want to intrude."

"It's not a problem. Mickey is going on this trip, to try to get some semi tankers for the Farm, for biodiesel storage. He should be able to get something going for you. Probably need to pay him some side money, though."

"Of course. Now the other part… Preparing for my old age. I've been thinking about that a lot during the winter. Do you think travel is going to become fairly commonplace again?"

"I don't think commonplace will be the word for it, but I'm banking on there being some, for my bar business."

"I'm thinking about gathering up the things needed for a small hotel. Just a few bedrooms, large lobby, and a dining room and kitchen. What do you think?"

"Your idea would be of much more benefit than my bar. I would only need one employee. You'd need three or four, at least. And having one available would probably draw people, though there are hundreds of abandoned rooms available for use, having the amenities will draw the high rollers. And it would probably be a cash business. Not too many people are going to traveling with a couple of chickens to trade for a good night's sleep."

Lucy laughed. "No. I suppose not. But don't be too sure. I guess only time will tell about where it should be, but I think I should start gathering good bedding and things like that, now."

"I think you should. As time passes, people are going to get used to abusing existing places, not bothering to maintain anything, since there 'will always be another'. And I doubt if we are the only ones scavenging. Things will eventually disappear. Or Mother Nature and wildlife will destroy them where they sit. Yep. Good idea."

"Your stuff wasn't all that bulky. What I'm going to be looking for will be. Mattresses and foundations and things like that. Plumbing fixtures. I want to have the amenities, like you said."

"We just hire one of the guys; maybe even two, to drive semis for our stuff, in addition to the Farms. Need someone to get a motor home back here for you, anyway."

"Oh. I guess I should warn you. You get the good stuff, but I'm going to use one of your ideas. I'm going to stock up on alcohol, too. The average stuff you don't want."

"Well," Jimmy laughed. "So much for my idea that we might be partners in the two endeavors. You'll be in partial competition with me."

Lucy managed a small smile, but her heart fell. He was probably serious about being partners. The two operations would go hand in hand. "Oh well," Lucy said lightly, despite her disappointment.

With most of the Farm's objectives preplanned, the scavenging went well, and it went fast. The last trailer load for the Farm went back in mid-July. Mickey and a married couple capable of driving semis stayed behind to help Jimmy and Lucy get a motorhome going for Lucy, and a semi- and two 53' reefer trailers for each of them.

Mickey headed back to the Farm, driving Lucy's new Class A motorhome, a gold eagle in his pocket for his services, which included not only getting it running and taking it to the Farm, but seeing to its hook up when he got it there. It would be ready for Lucy when she got back.

Both semis were big Kenworth over-the-road rigs with fancy sleepers. Charlene and Dwayne Cooper lived in one of them, while Lucy lived in the other, and Jimmy used his tent. The four spent the rest of the summer scavenging.

With no DOT rules to follow, the Coopers added another box trailer to the two on one of the Kenworths for their own scavenging efforts. Between them, Dwayne and Jimmy got a flatbed brick hauling trailer's hydraulic boom going. They attached it as third trailer to the other rig. Jimmy used it to get new electric forklift batteries and golf cart batteries for use with the solar panels and controllers they'd already scavenged, plus more they found at another big electrical warehouse. The batteries were dry, so Jimmy loaded up case after case of battery acid. They wouldn't add it to the batteries until they were eventually installed.

The trailers were full, as was the Suburban and another U-Haul trailer, well before harvest time. The group headed back to the Farm. Jimmy and Lucy were going to pay off the Coopers, but the husband and wife team declined, saying they'd found enough stuff scavenging to make up for the trip.

Since there was some summer left, Lucy and Jimmy decided to try the next city over. They would scavenge, but it would mostly be a scouting trip for the following year's efforts.

Taking another supply of PRI-D with them, they headed out in just the Suburban, with the intention of picking up another U-Haul trailer on the way. They got the last big tandem axle box trailer from the same U-Haul place, along with extra spare tires and headed for the second city.

There was a lot of stalled traffic on the Interstate from the war. There were no signs that anyone had traveled the road in years. They began sharing Jimmy's tent again, with no one else around, and a lack of other facilities.

When they got to the city they got a yellow pages phone book and headed for the high value places, including coin shops, gun dealers, and alcohol distributors.

Keeping the radiation survey meter handy at all times, and wearing dosimeters, they skirted the hot zone around the crater of the nuke that had taken out the east side of the city.

There were signs of scattered scavenging in the commercial areas, mostly food and liquor. There weren't many signs in the industrial areas they checked. They went back to a security routine due to the possibility of running into someone hostile to their efforts.

As they headed north to clear the hot zone, they ran into a residential area with lots of commercial establishments. Someone there took exception of their presence and fired three rounds at them. Either the person was a lousy shot, or they were intended as across-the-bows warning shots, for none hit the Suburban or trailer. Jimmy gunned the Suburban and turned around, to leave the area as quickly as possible.

"Time to head for home," Jimmy said. "Summer is about over, we're about maxed out in cargo capacity, and people are starting to shoot at us."

"No argument from me," Lucy replied. She had her AUG in her lap and the window down.

The harvest turned out to be a very good one, as summer lingered a bit longer than the current norm, and fall was mild, though short. The last of the oil crops for biodiesel were harvested in light snowfall.

Life at the farm settled into its winter routine. The only major change was Lucy moving into her motor home, and a few new babies on the scene. Lucy's former room in one of the Farm ranch houses was immediately put back into use by another female relative and her husband.

Lucy spent quite a bit of her time in Jimmy's motorhome, listening to his Yaesu VR-5000 broadband shortwave receiver, and getting his help in planning her small hotel. There seemed to be progress in many places around the country, and the world.

Lucy and Jimmy were both listening for clues to where the best place to set up shop in a few years might be.

If it was lunchtime or dinnertime, and Lucy was at Jimmy's, she usually fixed them a meal. Jimmy took her hunting occasionally, splitting the take three ways. One share for her, one for him, and one for the Farm. A couple of times they strapped on snowshoes, took full backpacks, and Jimmy's pulk, planning to stay out until they were able to get a couple of deer. They also saw coyote, wolf, wild dog, and puma tracks.

They were eminently successful, taking two deer in two days each time. One for the Farm and one for them to split. They saved a couple of good roasts from each of their deer, and made jerky strips from the rest of it. It took several days of working side-by-side, using an outside, wood fired smoke house/drying shed, to get it all done, but when they were finished, each had almost a full deer's worth of jerky.

Lucy showed Jimmy how to pressure can, using the equipment and supplies he'd scavenged on one of the trips, with the Ball Blue Book as his reference. He and Lucy always got a share of the community canned and preserved foods the Farm put by, for their help around the Farm, but preparing additional food was strongly encouraged.

The next summer was a near repeat of the previous one. Except Jimmy insisted they take a security team with them, as they would be going to the second city. It was well that Jimmy did. They were harassed the entire time they were in the northwest section of the city. Nobody was killed, but there were several bullet wounds, one serious. They picked up the things Jimmy and Lucy had located and got out of the area.

With things going well at the Farm, it was decided to cut the trip short, against Jimmy and Lucy's advice. Those with families declared it too dangerous to continue.

They were able to talk one un-attached younger man into staying with them and drive one of the three semis that had been put into service for the trip. Jimmy would drive the other one, and Lucy would drive the Suburban and the trailer they'd picked up in the new city. The group took the other one back to the Farm with what they had picked up so far.

Mark couldn't handle the truck with more than one trailer, so Jimmy sent him to the Farm with a trailer as soon as it was full, while he and Lucy continued the scavenging process, filling the next trailer while Mark was on his run.

Much to their surprise, they found a fuel distributor with plenty of fuel left. There were several tank trailers at the distributor and Jimmy filled all of them, and had Mark shuttle them back to the Farm, one at a time, despite the Farm having plenty of biodiesel. He had the PRI-D to rejuvenate it, and it was his and Lucy's, not the Farm's. They found another stock of both PRI-D and PRI-G at the distributors.

The city was larger than the first, and despite the fact that there were others scavenging, Jimmy and Lucy were able to safely acquire huge amounts of material for future use. Jimmy had become expert in getting into locked buildings, and Lucy was a whiz on a forklift. They found a diesel powered one that started right up and kept it with them when they moved.

SCAVENGER

Many things were loaded directly into the trailers with the forklift when a loading dock was available. Sometimes they had to move things from the pallet on the forklift at the rear of the trailer, to the front of the trailer and restack it on empty pallets; the loading still went much more quickly than previous expeditions.

For things too heavy to manhandle, Jimmy began using flat bed semi trailers, so Lucy could fully load them from the side. It was no problem getting tarps off other abandoned trucks to cover the loads. There was a greenhouse manufacturer in the city and Jimmy had Lucy load two flatbeds with the material to build several large greenhouses.

Mark brought back a friend that could drive and wanted to do some scavenging on his own. Moving the trailers caught up with Jimmy and Lucy's loading them.

Besides the stores and warehouses they were checking, Jimmy had started them checking semi loads abandoned on the road on the first scavenging trip. They'd recovered many things, but now, with the forklift and a pallet puller, they were able to get deep into those they couldn't before. They picked up an equipment trailer to carry the forklift with them.

One of the prized finds that would have been the Farm's, but became Jimmy's and Lucy's when the Farm opted out of the scavenging, was a double semi trailer load of Scott paper products, mostly toilet paper, but with plenty of paper towels and a couple of pallets of paper napkins. As long as they kept the trailers rodent free, they were set for life with toilet paper, even for their businesses, if they ever started up.

Mark and his friend had both gained enough experience to pull doubles, so the last loads went quickly as fall approached. One of the four trailers the two young men took back on their last trip was theirs. Unlike the Coopers, they accepted the payment Jimmy and Lucy gave them.

Jimmy didn't know what all they had scavenged, as they went through stuff after Jimmy and Lucy made their acquisition, but they seemed happy and were prepared to come back the next year.

Jimmy and Lucy stayed behind to fill two more semi-trailers, and the front of the equipment trailer, leaving just enough space to load the forklift. The Suburban and its trailer were, as usual, already filled with delicate and high value items.

The farm had another good fall and winter, and there were speculations that perhaps the harshest of the weather was behind them. Jimmy didn't think so. And said so. The weather always varied from norms, even severe ones.

When spring rolled around again, and another scavenging operation was organized, the Farm council called Jimmy and Lucy in to see them. Jimmy's little smile appeared, and Lucy looked glum when the council told them that there was concern about the amount of space their acquisitions were taking up, the time they were spending away from the farm, and that there was some jealousy about the possessions they were accumulating, even if it was not known exactly what they were.

After hesitating for a moment after Frank had stopped speaking, his wife, also a member of the council, cleared her throat and said, "Your relationship has become quite a disruptive topic of discussion and rumors."

Both Jimmy and Lucy started to speak, but Elizabeth held up her hand and continued speaking. "I know you have both stated, probably numerous times, that there is nothing more than a cooperative relationship between you.

"For this Farm to continue into the future it needs to expand and that means more people. Yes, you both do your share, but we need couples. Couples to bear children for the future."

Lucy turned pale and seemed to shrink into herself.

"You are both popular here and would have no trouble getting mates so you could settle down and raise families, if you truly aren't involved. If you are, you need to be married and not be living in sin. It gives the younger members of the Farm a bad impression."

Jimmy didn't argue the matter. He simply said, "I'll give you my decision when we get back from the scavenging trip."

Lucy's mind was a blank. All she could think of to say was, "Me, too."

As soon as they left the study in the main house, Jimmy said to Lucy, "I'm sorry I got you into this."

Lucy lifted her head. "I've been making my own decisions. I got myself into this. I'm just not sure how to get out of it."

"You don't have to make a decision right now. I wanted the time to think about it, and will, this summer."

"I'm too numb to think about it now, that's for sure."

They were both rather somber as the expedition headed out a few days later. But scavenging was exciting, and they soon were their old selves. Jimmy and Lucy had orders to send the Farm team back if they ran into gun trouble the way they had the previous year.

They were warned off a section of the city by another scavenging expedition. However it was by voice and not gunfire. Jimmy led them away, to another section of the city, telling the other group, "There's plenty for everyone."

And there was. The Farm made a good dent in their wish list, and Jimmy and Lucy were reaping in everything they could think of to set each of them up in business. Only Mark had been allowed to accompany Jimmy and Lucy for their part of the scavenging. His friend had been shifted to work only on the Farm's needs.

The summer didn't last long. The Farm people decided to go ahead and go back to the Farm, even though there were still items on the list. Jimmy and Lucy didn't object. Mark opted to go with them. He did agree to take back a set of doubles on the last trip for Jimmy and Lucy. He'd already shuttled six double trailer loads during the summer.

Jimmy and Lucy were relaxing in the tent after a hard day of manhandling goods they couldn't load with the forklift, the day after the others left. Jimmy had the phone book open, just thumbing through it. They had the next day planned out, but not the following days.

Something caught his eye, and he took a closer look at several ads. "Lucy, look at this," he said. She rolled over from her position on her stomach, having been writing in her journal.

"What is it?"

"What style of hotel did you have in mind?"

"None really. Not yet. I always just figured I'd have to use some suitable abandoned property when I found it."

"How about timber lodge style?" he showed her three ads in the yellow pages for log home and building companies."

"I never thought about it. I don't know. New construction?" Lucy looked up at Jimmy. "Lot of work."

"I'm sure we could get people to help. We're both in a position to pay for laborers. A lot of it depends on what they might have already prepared."

"Only way to find out is to go look."

A little reluctantly Jimmy left the tractor, partially loaded trailers, and forklift behind the next morning when they headed for the first of the locations outside the city. It was a big disappointment. They didn't have much there, and what was there had been burned almost to the ground.

They went to the second place, which was nearby. They were pleased with what they saw. There were a couple of display homes up, a couple with the parts bundled and ready for shipment, two more partially assembled in their test run, and both the processed and raw log yards were nearly full. So was the warehouse where things like trim, windows, and doors were stored. The place looked to have been abandoned right after the war.

Despite how good it looked, they decided to check the other place out as well. They couldn't even get close. There was an armed guard at the turn off up to the company site. They weren't threatened, but they were told in no uncertain terms that the place was off limits to them unless they were related to the owners.

Jimmy turned the Suburban around and headed back to the second place. They took their time going through the offices, matching the brochures to the display homes, the ones packed for shipping, and the ones under construction. None of them were really suitable for either Jimmy's or Lucy's plans. But there were hundreds of logs ready to be cut to length for use in the building process. Each building was designed, cut, and assembled prior to the pieces being numbered, and then dismantled and packed for shipment.

The place must have been booming before the war shut it down. They found a dozen orders for homes and buildings in the offices, besides the two being cut, and the two ready for shipment.

"We take it all," Jimmy said, "except for the standing units. There is more than enough for both of us to build much larger places than we were wanting."

"It seems overwhelming. How are we going to get it back to the farm, much less to the final destination? The Farm doesn't even really want us bringing back more stuff."

"Where there is a will, there is a way. Personally, I am feeling somewhat unwelcome at the Farm at the moment. I'm ready to start moving lock, stock, and barrel to here, until we decide where each one of us wants to go permanently."

"I can't say I disagree," Lucy said slowly. "But what about security? We are safe at the Farm."

"I think we can get a few people from the area surrounding the farm to come along and set up a compound..." After a pause, Jimmy added, "but it sure would be better if we just went ahead and took everything to the final destinations."

"I just simply don't know," Lucy said.

"Well," Jimmy said, looking off to the west, "I'm seriously considering the Mississippi River. From some of the radio traffic, it's clear that it is a major transportation route, just like it always has been. People are on the river constantly. And you've got I-55 going north and south along it. I'm thinking a place where the river and the interstate are close, would be ideal, especially if there is an existing landing, or I could manage to get one put in, somehow."

"Sounds like you've given this a lot more thought than I have," Lucy replied.

"Actually, it's only come to me recently, when we were listening to the shortwave radio. You know… If it would be good for my business, it would probably be good for yours. We could actually be partners. Simplify a lot of things."

Jimmy was astounded when Lucy looked forlorn and started to cry.

"Lucy? What is it, Lucy? Why are you crying?"

"Don't you get it, Jimmy? I've fallen in love with you. I don't want a business partner. I want a lover and a helpmeet. A husband."

"Holy cow!" Jimmy said. He took her into his arms, without a protest from her and let her cry on his shoulder for a while. When the sobs stopped, Jimmy stepped back, took her chin in his hand and lifted it so he could look into her eyes.

"You've been driving me crazy almost since the day I met you. You don't know how hard it's been to keep my feelings to myself. You had made it clear you didn't want children. To me that goes with not having a husband."

"Oh, Jimmy, I am afraid to have children, because of my first failure. And I know you like children. I've never allowed myself to think you'd want to be with someone that couldn't bear you children."

"Oh, I'd like to have children, but it isn't the highest priority. Having someone intelligent and capable by my side is what I want. Being beautiful would be a plus. You are definitely that, even in silk long johns or a man's tee-shirt and boxers.'

"Oh, Jimmy, I…"

Jimmy cut Lucy's words off when he hugged her to him and kissed her for a very long time. It was already late in the day. The two silently set up the tent and entered. They shared a sleeping bag that night, and it wasn't because it was cold.

With new perspectives, the two got up the next morning to approach the day. They had a quick breakfast and then got ready to leave the property, rather reluctantly. When they got into the Suburban to leave, Jimmy opened the special electrical switch panel and took out what was obviously a ring case.

"This is the first thing I saw when we started scavenging for the good stuff. I thought of you when I saw it. Will you marry me?"

With shaking hands Lucy opened the ring box. It was an exquisite two carat marquise diamond in a simple platinum setting, with a half carat brilliant cut diamond on each side. Jimmy reached over, took the ring out of the case and slipped it on Lucy's left hand ring finger.

"Well?" Jimmy said softly.

"Yes," replied Lucy, just as softly. She leaned over and Jimmy kissed her again. Then he put the Suburban in gear and they headed back to the scavenged items that they'd left behind.

SCAVENGER

Rather on pins and needles the entire time, hoping no one else would discover the treasure trove of building materials they had, Jimmy and Lucy continued to scavenge in the second city until the weather turned on them.

One of the semi tractors they had available had an automatic transmission. Jimmy worked with Lucy for a couple of days while it was raining. When they hooked up the trailers, Jimmy and Lucy were both confident that she could get the rig back to the Farm, if they went slowly. And that was with a whopping four trailers each. The Suburban and trailer were loaded onto the equipment trailer behind the forklift.

Lucy was pulling three flatbeds and the equipment trailer, since they would catch the least wind. Jimmy had four 53' reefers, though they weren't running the cooling units. They wanted the trailers for future use.

When they got to the road up to the Farm, they unhooked down to two trailers each, and went up to drop them, before going back down to get the other four. There were some sour faces on the Farm's council when they saw the eight final trailers.

Jimmy went up to them and said, "We both intend leave in the spring, with all our gear. Hopefully, we can stay the winter. We're willing to pay for it if you want us to. And Lucy and I plan to be married at the upcoming Christmas wedding feast."

Most of the council were shaking their heads and saying that they didn't need to leave if they were getting married. That they had a lot to offer the community. That they didn't need to pay. Frank's wife was the only one that still had a sour look.

Jimmy and Lucy fell into the same winter routine they'd developed, except Lucy was now sharing Jimmy's motorhome and his bed. During that winter they talked to one of the family members that had architectural training and worked up a set of plans for a small hotel and tavern, to be built of double T&G logs curved on the outside face and square on the inside face.

Though he was unlicensed, Jimmy fired up his own Yaesu Amateur Radio rig and went on a fact finding mission via the airwaves. He talked to people up and down the Mississippi from St. Louis to Memphis.

Though many people tried to talk the pair out of leaving, now that they were married, Jimmy and Lucy were adamant about leaving. They headed toward southern Illinois after having considered many recommendations and requests for them to come to specific places on the river.

Despite no longer being active when the war started, Whiteman Air Force Base on the western side of Missouri had taken many nuclear hits on the empty missile silos located there. Fallout had been heavy all across mid- and southern Missouri. Targets in Arkansas had added additional fallout.

But there were many farms and a few ranches on both sides of the Mississippi near Cairo, Illinois area that had been able to protect much of their livestock, and had decontaminated many of the tillable fields for crops. There was a resource base available to support the area, including the businesses Jimmy and Lucy planned.

Another resource was the River traffic going up and down the Missouri, the Mississippi, and the Ohio.

SCAVENGER

The Missouri joined the Mississippi, and the Ohio joined at Cairo, Illinois. Cairo had several River traffic businesses so there would be plenty of River users with whom to do business, plus the local population.

I-55 was suffering the ravages of nature, including those of one large earthquake not long after the war. There were some efforts to keep it useable, since it was the primary land link from the Gulf of Mexico to north of St. Louis. Not much was done north of St. Louis. It was the point where year round snow was accumulating into the makings of future glaciers.

As soon as they got there, Jimmy and Lucy fell in love with the place. One of the first things they did upon arriving was to contact the local security people, which turned out to be relatively intact State Patrol and County Sheriff's Deputies in the area. With their help, Jimmy and Lucy got a small security force together to make sure nothing they brought to the area was taken from them on the way, or when it got there.

Jimmy also had to make arrangements to have a proxy collect the rent from his properties, convert it to gold, and send it to him.

All those arrangements made, and a piece of abandoned property selected, Jimmy and Lucy began supervising the daunting task of transporting all their belongings from the Farm to just south of Cairo. They had ten long haul semi tractors, plus one trip with the yard ruck to move the dozens of semi-trailers Jimmy and Lucy had accumulated, plus the many loads of timbers and other building materials from the log home builder. They decided to take the un-worked timbers, too. If nothing else they could be used for firewood.

Besides gold and silver coins, there was a brisk trade in quality jewelry. They'd been prepared to pay in gold and silver coins, but since people were willing to take jewelry, they were more than happy to oblige. The move cost most of the contents of one large jewelry store, but Jimmy and Lucy had that and more, due to their foresight.

They even picked up some things along the way on the first two trips, stopping and checking the semis abandoned on the roads between the Farm and Cairo. Most of the small towns either had been picked clean, or the locals warned them off trying to scavenge there.

Jimmy and Lucy decided to buy fuel from the Farm for the move, since the farm had it to spare, and they wanted to keep what they'd accumulated for a rainy day. Someone was supposed to be making biodiesel around Cairo, but they had yet to find whoever it was.

The move was completed before fall. That included using stock trailers to move the small herd of Angus cattle and bison Jimmy had been trading for over the years. There was plenty of beef around Cairo, but Jimmy had the herd and knew it was prime quality so moved it instead of trading it off at the Farm. Bison was unheard of in the area and would be a specialty at the hotel dining room. Jimmy's small herd of horses was also moved.

A local farmer eagerly accepted management of the herds for stud services from the Angus bulls, plus a couple of cows out of the first birthing the next spring, with the understanding that the beef and bison would be only for the hotel's use. Jimmy and Lucy wouldn't go into direct competition with him.

The farmer had a small Angus herd himself, but only had one bull. His herd needed new blood desperately. He would also provide pork and chicken for the hotel kitchen, as well as dairy items.

Another farmer took possession of two of the large greenhouses and a generator for the grow lights, in return for the pick of the crop for the hotel. The farmer could sell the remainder of the crop.

One of the things they'd been uncertain about was the matter of a good foundation for their new building, but there had been quite a bit of barge traffic of Portland cement on the river and they were able to get all they needed to put a full basement under the structure. Plenty of aggregate was available, too. The basement for the hotel and several other buildings on the property were made with very good concrete, after Jimmy paid a local contractor with a working excavator to dig them and run the concrete mixer they traded for locally.

The basement and foundation walls were extra wide, for Jimmy and Lucy had learned that the winters in the area were even more severe than what they were experienced with, though with slightly less snow, but much more wind.

Since they had plenty of the machined logs, the exterior walls of the building would be doubled, with a space between, protected by plastic sheeting. The foam board they had originally, reluctantly, planned to put on the inside of the log wall and finish conventionally, would go on the inside of the outer wall, and the space between the walls filled with eighteen inches of earth for a heat sink. They would be able to have the machined log interior.

The roof was of enameled metal, on a 12/12 pitch. It allowed plenty of room for two feet of insulation on the ceiling, assuring a warm building with minimal use of firewood for heating. It would also keep the building cooler in the summer time.

Jimmy and Lucy had thoroughly discussed the amounts they would pay for various services in and around Cairo, on the trip from the Farm to Cairo with the first trailer loads of material.

They would be demanding a very high standard of work, which would naturally cost more than standard wages in the area. But they didn't want to artificially inflate Cairo's local economy, and raise the cost to themselves needlessly. They asked around when they got back to Cairo on that trip and got a general feel for what things went for in the area. Then they set up wage scales and equivalencies for those that still didn't trust gold and silver, much less jewelry.

With law enforcement active in the area, and with their being on site full time, Jimmy and Lucy let the security team go. They wound up hiring most of them back as laborers for the construction work that would be done before winter set in.

The construction that was done, besides the basements and foundations, was to get two more of the greenhouses set up. One would provide flowers and specialty foods for the hotel and tavern. The other would be a solarium and winter heat source for the hotel. It was situated so it could always be used for growing things if it became necessary. Actually, until the hotel was finished, it would be used to get plants started in pots, which would eventually adorn the solarium and some of the lobby areas of the hotel itself.

They had brought pipe and well points with them. There was no trouble getting one of the former well drillers in the area to get their rig going long enough to drill a new deep well for the hotel. Ditto the sewer system, except for the septic tank, which was cast in place in with more concrete.

The support structures for solar panels were installed, and a few panels put up, to provide electrical power for the motor home they would be living in that winter. More would be added during the construction of the hotel.

Jimmy and Lucy settled in for the winter. And indeed it was a bad one. They were further south than they had been, further from the line just north of St. Louis that marked the limit of continual snow accumulation.

Word began to spread of the proposed new business, both up and down the river, and all around the area on both sides of it.

When spring rolled around, the few people that were traveling made stops to find out if the rumors were true, and if so, when the establishment would open. Neither Jimmy nor Lucy would give definitive answer, but suggested that people check the coming fall.

Construction started as soon as it was warm enough to be sure the weather would not adversely affect the process. There was no shortage of workers, many who negotiated with Jimmy and Lucy to get food during the winter for their families, with a reduced rate of pay during the summer.

Jimmy and Lucy were eager to agree. Food should not be a problem for them. They had all the labor they needed, allowing several sets of laborers to be working at the same time on different sections of the structure.

Lucy had read up on hotel design and operations in several of the huge number of books that Jimmy had. Since the bulk of the business would be the hotel, Lucy took charge of supervising its construction, with Jimmy only concerning himself with the tavern that would be part of the hotel, and overall supervision of the building processes.

People came to watch the process, with observers there almost every day construction went on. Many of them seemed fascinated with what would come out of the fleet of semi-trailers belonging to Jimmy and Lucy. There was even a running gamblers' pool on it.

Jimmy also took care of several new businesses that they developed due to circumstances. They leased many of the trailers out as they were emptied, to the river boat operations. Since Jimmy had always taken a reefer trailer if it was available, over a regular box trailer, he and Lucy had plenty of the diesel powered cooling unit reefers to go around. It opened up the transport of some perishable cargo that previously had been very small scale operations.

There was still plenty of diesel around, in tank farms along the Mississippi, though its age was giving the tug operators some problems. Jimmy guaranteed the reefers would run if he provided the fuel, for which he charged significantly extra, but he wouldn't fuel the tugs. It would deplete his stock of PRI-D much too fast. The semi tractors he kept local, for fear of losing control of them.

The reefers were also useful for storing the perishables when the shipments that came to Cairo got there. He kept the reefers in storage use on their property. He wouldn't allow the owners of the products take them to their own places, again for fear of losing possession, possession being nine-tenths of the law, especially now.

The greenhouses had been planted after being installed the previous year and were producing well. Since they didn't need it themselves at the moment, Jimmy dried some of it and sold the rest to the locals.

With the construction going so well, they gave everyone a paid day off on July 4th, and sponsored a celebration. It was well received and helped cement the Holden's place in the community.

The exterior work was finished shortly after the 4th of July celebration, and finish work began inside. The rest of the site work started as well.

A full complement of photovoltaic panels was installed, with attendant controllers and two battery banks. With them on line, they had 75% power continuously, with battery back up at the same rate for seven days. Much longer at reduced loads.

But Jimmy had acquired several diesel generators during the scavenging expeditions. There were four identical 21kw diesel units that Jimmy had in mind from the start for such an application he was now putting them to.

One would run 75% of the electrical draw of the complex alone, if the solar panels weren't working, and would kick in if more than the 75% the solar panels would furnish was needed. Two would furnish 100% of the complex electrical needs, running at half load. A third would be on standby to start up if one of the others went down, and during servicing of the units when 100% power was need. The fourth was essentially a spare. It would go into the cycle when it was time to rebuild one of the generators.

Jimmy had service components and rebuild kits to keep the four generators running for years. There were also additional photovoltaic panels and controllers and components, for replacement and for additional installations.

Part of the power generation plan was to draw fuel from the semi tank trailers. Three could be hooked up, to be pulled from in sequence, with a loaded replacement being always available. The fifteen loaded tanks they still had would run them for years as long as the photovoltaics carried most of the load.

After currently stored fuel ran out they would use biodiesel. They were already getting one tank trailer filled for other uses. They wanted to set up a routine of use so the farmer would maintain production, if not increase it for the time when everyone was dependent on the biodiesel.

Finally, the landscaping was done, and then the interior work. Summer was rapidly fading as the installation of the furniture was begun, as well as stocking the storage rooms from the goods in the trailers. Lucy began interviewing people for the positions the establishment would need. She let Jimmy look for the small staff he needed for the tavern.

They began to announce the Grand Opening for September 1st over the radio networks the area used, and by word of mouth. When the day rolled around, it was a disappointing turn out. Quite a few locals showed up for the free food and drinks, but no river people showed up at all.

Lucy managed not to cry, but it was a near thing as she began to wrap up things for the evening. But as she was about to dismiss everyone, the door opened again and six people came in. Lucy smiled and greeted them, as she was acting as hostess for the Grand Opening.

"We're the crew of the Molly Jo," said the obvious leader of the group. "I'm Captain Johanson. Hear you have buffalo meat. Haven't had that in some time. Been a long time between good beds, too. Can you feed us and put us up for the night?"

"We certainly can," Lucy said. She extended one arm toward the dining room. "This way to the dining room." Lucy grabbed six simple menus that she'd printed up on Jimmy's computer and printer and guided the men to a large table. Her lone busboy was there immediately, to fill water glasses. Missy, one of the three waitresses that Lucy had hired was right there, too.

"Enjoy your meal," Lucy said. "Afterwards just come to the lobby and we'll check you in." She was smiling. "And the meal, as you are our first customers, will be on the house. Drinks excepted."

"Why, we weren't expecting that!" said the Captain. "Thank you very much. Rumor has it you have a real bar with real liquor. Would that be a fact?"

"It is, sir. We have quite a selection, as a matter of fact. Feel free to order a drink here at the table, or spend some time in the tavern before you retire."

"Count on it," Captain Johanson said. "We're here for a couple of days for repairs."

The following morning a few locals showed up for coffee. They were limited to two cups apiece, but for such a rare commodity, the price the dining room was charging was quite reasonable, especially since one of the payment options was half an hour's labor for the two cups. The labor was mostly for wood cutting along the river to provide firewood for the three fireplaces and several wood stoves in the hotel and tavern.

It was a slow start, but as the word spread, they began to get more and more business. Not only were they the only real game in town, they were the best game, offering the best available food and lodging in a very large area.

The country began to make a comeback, the pockets of civilization like the Farm and Cairo becoming the new centers of trade. There was a heavy migration to the south as the winters stayed severe and the summer's mild, making it difficult to grow enough food to sustain the population in the north.

Much of the transport was of food. The fields of central Missouri, and western Kansas could still produce wheat. It was trucked to the Missouri, and then went on riverboats east to the Mississippi and then south. Products of the south went north and then east on the Ohio, and west on the Missouri. The coal operations in the Ohio valley were managing to stay in operation, with the new old market for heating coal, rather than electrical generation.

Only a few of the tugboats would take barges past St. Louis, to the Missouri River. St. Louis had been hit with three nukes during the war, and all the bridges were down, plus there was a new Lake St. Louis where one of the devices had detonated almost right on the river. The crater filled rapidly. Though the water itself did not become radioactive, it was a hot spot that had to be crossed to go west on the Missouri. There wasn't much need to go further north on the

Mississippi. The river was coming from beneath the beginning glacier several miles north of St. Louis.

Due to the hot spot in the river, there was a small business going to truck around St. Louis from the Mississippi to the Missouri.

Cairo was around the midpoint of the run from Kansas to the Gulf, and Ohio to the Gulf. Soon they had several regular river people stopping in for a break from their routine. Because ground transportation was limited because of fuel availability, many people in the surrounding countryside began coming to the river ports on their own, to pick up supplies. They found a comfortable, convenient place to lay over at Holden's before their return trip home with their load of supplies.

Again, with the shortage and expense of fuel, many people had taken to horses to provide transportation. Even quite a few of the tugboats began keeping horses on board for transportation ashore when docked. Jimmy had foreseen that, and one of the buildings on the complex was a stable for guests' horses.

There was also a row of hitching posts in front of the taverns separate outside entrance. Jimmy kept a couple of horses trained for harness and a locally acquired horse drawn surrey at the stable with a driver for guest's use.

Business was slow, but sure. The Holden's were breaking even, taking in about the equivalent of what they were having to purchase. Their herds; cattle, bison, and horses; were increasing nicely. They were using up stored consumables for which there were no replacements available, but even of those, they still had several years' worth in storage.

The compound was a tempting target for those eager to gain at the end of a gun. Jimmy and Lucy always went armed with at least a handgun, and several of the employees did so, as well. The double barrel whippet shotgun Jimmy had liberated was in a prominent position on the back bar in the tavern. There was also a Remington 11-87 police shotgun under the bar, out of sight.

Though there were three hold up attempts the first full summer of operation, all were stopped in their tracks, with a couple of robbers killed, a couple wounded, and half a dozen or more run off or captured by local law enforcement.

Holden's gained a reputation of being a good place to deal with, but not one to mess with. Both reputations were fine with Jimmy and Lucy.

CHAPTER SIX

When winter came that year, it came even earlier than usual, but was mild compared to the recent winters.

Though the Missouri froze over, the Mississippi stayed clear of thick ice somewhat south of St. Louis. Cairo became the turnaround point for river traffic during the winter, so Holden's maintained their slow, steady business.

With things going so well, Jimmy and Lucy began feeling the wanderlust when spring rolled around. They had a well-trained and seasoned staff now, and local law enforcement officers were regulars at the hotel and dining room. Jimmy and Lucy decided to see what St. Louis had to offer scavengers willing to risk moderate radiation exposure.

They hooked up two box trailers, a flatbed trailer, and the equipment trailer to the best of the Kenworth OTR semi tractors with sleeper. The Suburban, forklift, and four 55-gallon drums of diesel were loaded onto the equipment trailer. They set off for St. Louis one dry, blustery, spring day. They would live in the sleeper, rather than camp out. It was equipped with a chemical toilet and a microwave, as well as the bed.

There was no need to bother with any of the few remaining semis abandoned on I-55. Everything between St. Louis and the Gulf had been scavenged if it was the least bit usable. So had the outskirts of St. Louis, at least on the southern end. But as they began to enter areas where the radiation was much above 0.1R/hr, there was significantly less scavenging evident. They began to check things out, yellow pages in hand.

They followed their standard procedures, looking for high value items, primarily, and taking anything else that might turn a coin if they found it. One of the things they had not run across in the other cities was a furrier. They loaded up dozens of good fur coats and other garments.

The fuel distributors they could get to had pretty much been cleaned out. Apparently not that many people knew the benefits of PRI-D, or had taken the fuel early on when it was still fresh. They found a lifetime supply of PRI-D and PRI-G, between the three distributors they hit.

St. Louis also had quite a few gun shops and several distributors. Most of the gun shops and a couple of the distributors had been picked over heavily. Jimmy and Lucy took everything that was left, and cleaned out the distributors that still had their full inventory.

They never did take the Suburban off the equipment trailer, but they did load it up with the things they didn't want to lose if they had to make a run for it. They thought they might as they finished cleaning out the last of the gun distributors warehouses.

SCAVENGER

They came under rifle fire right after Lucy loaded and chained down the forklift. They fired back, each dumping three thirty round magazines into the area from which the fire had come. They ran for the truck. It was always parked headed in a safe direction and left idling while the trailers were loaded. Jimmy only had to put it in gear. They heard two more shots, but when they inspected everything later they found some scratch marks on the flatbed that might have been made by bullets, but nothing seemed to be damaged.

Except for Jimmy. He had groove cut in his left thigh. As soon as they got far enough away, Lucy tended to him, having a difficult time from the tears in her eyes. But they had an excellent first-aid kit, including a trauma dressing with blood stopper. They also had a good selection of pain killers. She gave Jimmy one after she'd bandaged his leg and had him lie down in the sleeper.

Though she had to go really slow, with the four trailers, Lucy headed them south, toward Cairo. The trailers were nearly full anyway. They had made a very good haul. Their scavenging was done, at least for the moment, if not permanently, Lucy decided.

When they got back late summer, things were going well at the compound. Slow steady business. The staff had done well on their own, and were each given a paid day off, at one end or the other of their regular two days off, in rotation, for their good work.

Early one afternoon shortly after they got back, Jimmy and Lucy were sitting at one of the tables in the tavern, having tea and coffee respectively when Captain Johanson came in with his crew. "You're back," he said. "Been waiting all summer to talk to you."

"Pull up a chair," Jimmy said, waving Mike, the day bartender, over to take the Captain's drink order as the rest of the crew lined up at the bar.

"What's up?" Jimmy asked.

"Got another proposition for you." Johanson was one of the tugboat captains using the Holden reefers for perishable goods.

"I'm listening," Jimmy said.

Johanson pulled a cigar from inside his jacket. "Try this." He handed Jimmy the cigar.

"I'm not a smoker," Jimmy replied.

"Oh." Johanson's face fell. "I was thinking you might want to sell these here in the tavern. Tobacco is hard to come by, and well… I have a source for these in Cuba and thought they might go over pretty good here, with the fine liquors and stuff."

"Cubans, huh?" Jimmy said, picking up the cigar and running it under his nose. "Nice aroma. How many and how much?"

Lucy laughed and left the two to work out the details. She knew her husband well. He sensed a profitable deal.

Premium cigars were available for those that had the money and wanted one. Cheaper ones were available for those that just wanted a smoke. Johanson was going to check to see if his supplier could get good pipe tobacco. If so, it would be added to the inventory.

His next trip up river he stopped in again and delivered two crates of cigars and pipe tobacco. He would be paid in services at the tavern. Jimmy made out like a bandit. Tobacco was indeed rare, and much sought after.

Other people began to come to the Holden's with similar deals. Jimmy made one for South American coffee, but the guy couldn't come through. Fortunately, with the way they rationed it, their supply would last for several years, but they would like to find a replacement supply. Some entrepreneur would eventually open up a good link.

With a more distant time in mind, Lucy had included in the lobby what in the old days would have been a gift shop. She began to put special items they'd acquired specifically for trade or sale on the shelves and racks and began to get another income stream started. As fall approached, she began displaying a couple of the furs they'd scavenged. They went quickly.

But a local trapper came to her and said he could provide fur apparel as well, made from the local animals he trapped. She put him on a consignment basis. His less expensive line of warm winter wear also moved well. Lucy got a small commission on each sale, and the trapper had a much better place in which to sell his goods, than his little cabin or on the streets.

Though they had fresh fish from the Mississippi, Lucy eagerly made a deal with another of the tugboat captains to provide seafood from the Gulf. She provided him one of the diesel powered reefer trailers in which to transport it during the summer. She already had two of the reefers dismounted from the running gear, attached to the kitchen area of the hotel for her own cold storage. They were plumbed in to the same diesel supply feeding the generators.

There was a huge demand for salt, for preserving meat and for seasoning. Jimmy made a similar deal with the Captain to obtain salt from one of the entrepreneurs on the Gulf coast that had begun making salt from seawater.

The previous winter had been milder than the new norm. The current winter turned out to be much worse than the new norm. The Ohio and Mississippi rivers were covered with thick ice. The Ohio to where it joined the Mississippi, and the Mississippi to just north of Cairo. Large chunks of ice floated past the city regularly during the winter.

Jimmy, while he was recuperating from his leg wound had studied up on the weather. With a fancy Davis weather instrument set and a computer, he became the local weatherman. He forecast a big blizzard right after Thanksgiving. He was right.

The Holden's opened up the hotel and tavern to those that had inadequate shelter that could get there. They saved quite a few lives those four days. Many of the people that came to the compound would not have survived otherwise.

When they began to dig out and go back to their own homes many bodies were found frozen to death. Temperatures had been down to fifty below a couple of the nights of the blizzard. The hotel/tavern was the only really warm place in the area. A few people brought in things to repay the Holden's the next summer for their generosity during the blizzard, but they were a definite minority.

But Jimmy and Lucy endured. For the times, they were fabulously wealthy, due to their work, and the risks they took, in the years since the war. They did not make it obvious how wealthy they truly were. Many of the semi-trailers in the compound lot were known to be empty. No one besides the Holden's knew how many were still full. Trailers were only unloaded at night, under cover of darkness. Or how much of the weather sensitive stuff had been moved to the basements of the various buildings right after they were built, when there was a lot of activity going on.

But you can never be too wealthy, especially in hard times. And the times were still hard. Jimmy and Lucy made it less hard for others, due to the services and goods they supplied. But there always seemed to be another problem, around another bend.

Such was the case with the new 1920's style gangsters that began making their presence known. A cross section of American society had survived the war. That included gang members. Many died, just as members of other segments of society did, with the coming of the new ice age. There was much free for the taking, and many people survived on what they found in the homes and businesses near them.

But such easy supplies don't last forever. As more and more people began to recover and become productive again, those who's past had included preying on the weak and unprepared began to do so again. It was small at first, and then they learned, from people with more experience, some of the more violent ways to make a living.

Where the Holden's had suffered attempted robberies before, they had been transients or the bad element of the locals. Very small groups. The rumors came up from the south, where life was a bit easier. There were gangsters going into towns, shooting them up, and taking whatever they wanted. That included women, girls, men and boys. There was a new international trade in slaves. It wasn't black slavery, or white slavery, or Hispanic slavery. It was non-racial slavery. Mostly the women and girls for sex, and the men and boys as laborers, but that was by no means always the case.

Many of the less developed nations had always been dependent on their large populations for a labor force. As warlords came to power in those areas, they wanted and needed more labor to maintain their lifestyles. Many just liked it. Others used their own people as soldiers, and the slaves for work.

MS-13 was said to be behind much of the slave trade in the US, but there was obviously more than one gang doing it. There were too many reports from too many areas for there not to be. And there had to be a market.

While Jimmy and Lucy were known to take calculated risks, they didn't take chances. Most of their staff was furnished with weapons, and a few security people were hired. Everyone in the area was cautioned to be on their guard and to report to the local authorities any unknown groups of people, or individuals acting suspiciously.

As was usual with new dangers, people watched out for them religiously for a while, and when nothing happened, became lax about security. Such was the case in Cairo. Only a handful, including the Holden's, maintained their higher state of alert. It was well they did, for an unknown tugboat with four barges docked at the Cairo docks one late fall day.

No one at Cairo ever knew just how many men there were, but there were enough to leave a heavily armed force on the tugboat and barges to protect them while two other groups stormed the town. One group headed directly for the Holden's place.

Jimmy and Lucy had about ten minutes notice that an attack was underway before the MS-13 gangsters showed up. They were met with withering fire from the buildings in the complex. Jimmy had told his employees no mercy since there would be none in return.

When the rumors had first started, Jimmy had pulled out of storage some of the weapons they had scavenged; particularly those from the two class three licensed places. He didn't much care for full auto fire, except for static defense and ambushes. But it was as effective as he knew it would be when he and the employees poured round after round into the approaching group.

They quickly dispersed, but the first bursts of fire had severely reduced their number. Jimmy had ammunition to burn, and burn it they did. With the full auto suppressive fire coming from several of the employees, Jimmy and a Deputy Sheriff that happened to be there advanced and began rooting out individual attackers.

The firing around the compound died down and those defending it heard the firing coming from other areas of the town. With the few live gangsters under armed guard, the men at the compound headed out to help in the other battles.

When it was all said and done, thirty-seven gangsters were killed, wounded, or captured. Six townspeople had died, with another eleven wounded, three seriously. No one was taken by the few gangsters that escaped.

Jimmy and the Deputy were both on the wounded list. Deputy Roberts had a round shatter the bone in his upper left arm. He would probably lose the arm.

Jimmy had another leg wound, this one much more serious than the crease he'd received before. The bullet went into his left leg from slightly to his right, nicking the bone before it stopped.

He was in surgery for two hours while the bullet was removed, and the damage sewn up. The Deputy was still in surgery when Lucy went back to the compound to take care of things there. Jimmy would be in the hospital for several days.

The Deputy was lucky that several of the doctors in St. Louis, when the war broke out, came to Cairo and had brought equipment and supplies with them. They couldn't save the Deputy's arm, but they did save his life.

Captain Johanson reported six days later that he and six other tugboats had cornered and blocked the gangster's tugboat and barges. The gangsters slaughtered the slaves they'd already collected. None of the gangsters survived, either.

The defeat of the gangsters at Cairo broke the back of the organization in the area. It was a long time before other areas were able to free themselves from the tyranny that the gangsters represented. The gangsters were one reason that more people were moving into the area around Cairo, or stopped there permanently on their migration south.

When Jimmy got out of the hospital he was more than a little annoyed that the city and county officials had claimed everything from the gangsters' side of the fight, including the tugboat and barges. He was used to claiming the spoils of war when he was victorious in battle. He pestered the officials into giving him a share of what was taken, and traded for a few choice items that he wanted. It soothed some of the pain in his leg.

SCAVENGER

Gold coins, specifically the one-ounce gold ones, had become the new monetary standard for most of the existing civilizations around the world. Even nay-sayers and critics of gold had to begin using it. The standard was the one ounce coins, but fractional gold coins and pre-1965 US silver coins were used for most transactions.

Much trading and bartering continued, but travelers needed portable currency, and very small transactions were difficult to make without using silver dimes and quarters. Large transactions weren't as big of a problem, but many people just preferred the gold and silver.

With there being an accepted standard, trade was much easier, especially international trade. There wasn't much of it, but what was being shipped back and forth was all very highly valued, with much of it critical items like basic foods.

But it meant transportation had to be available. And that meant major expenses. Other things began to have standard values, based on gold. That included investment grade diamonds.

As has been the case throughout history, some people became wealthy, like the Holden's, through hard work, good planning, and some luck. It was true around the world. And the wealthy wanted extraordinary or special things. And could afford them.

The average person wanted water, food, shelter, and protection. With much of the European and Russian breadbaskets under growing sheets of ice, and the population dropping in it, the central portion of the US again became the breadbasket to much of the remainder of the western world. But it needed to be shipped to ports in Europe.

Between the fact that many of the ports on the east coast were radioactive hot spots, and the fact that a large portion of the grain was grown west of the Mississippi, and only a few good crossing points still existed, the Gulf ports supplied by the Mississippi barge traffic became the shipping and receiving points of choice for European, Mediterranean, North African and Russian markets.

A ship that could carry tons of grain could easily turn an unused cabin or other ship's space into a small hold to carry the relatively small sized, highly profitable specialty items.

And European entrepreneurs seemed to like diamonds much more than even gold for their large transactions. Diamond jewelry was second choice to investment diamonds, but Jimmy was able to use the bulk of their scavenged jewelry to get set up in European based international trade of cattle; grain; coal; oil; and spices and other low volume, high value, specialty items. He would hold onto the good diamonds for less risky deals.

Jimmy and Lucy held interest in six small dry cargo vessels and two small tankers. With the Gulf oil production starting to come back, it was more profitable to sell a tanker load to Europe than distribute it around the US. The interior of the US would need to rely on biodiesel for the foreseeable future.

The Holden's took their profits half in gold and half in goods. What goods they didn't use, and they used very little, were resold. But there was a limited market in Cairo, even including the surrounding area.

They needed to expand their market for specialty items.

Jimmy began to make more contacts on the Amateur Radio network that was the primary form of communication around the world. He was able to set up deals with several like-minded entrepreneurs to handle distribution. The main drawback was transportation from Cairo to the other centers of civilization.

But where there is a need, someone usually comes up with a solution. Sure enough, during Jimmy's search for markets of his goods, he made contact with a compound with a large biodiesel operation, which could provide fuel for its small fleet of diesel cars and trucks. They were already in the transport business. Jimmy made the deal to use them for his transport company.

Cairo became the major center of trade for the central United States. The Holden's efforts had much to do with it, but the country as a whole was beginning to make a comeback, the small centers of civilization that had been the initial survivors began to expand into the abandoned areas.

With small and large farms springing up everywhere the weather allowed, and an electrical power plant here and there being put back into service, even small towns that had only a few individuals surviving in them began to get more residents as new job opportunities opened up and retail food became available from the local farms.

With the growing population, it was inevitable that central government would once again come into existence. It was true around the world. For most, it seemed like the world might return to some semblance of normal. Jimmy and Lucy began looking for new cache places.

The End

***THANK YOU FOR READING**_

"SCAVENGER"

By

Jerry D. Young

LIKE THIS BOOK?

See more great books at www.creativetexts.com

"OZARK RETREAT"

"BUGGING HOME"

"THE SLOW ROAD"

"LOW PROFILE"

"RUDY'S PREPAREDNESS SHOP"

"CME: CORONAL MASS EJECTION"

"HOME SWEET BUNKER"

"THE HERMIT"

& MANY MORE GREAT PAW FICTION & OTHER TITLES

THANK YOU!

MEET THE AUTHOR

Jerry D Young was born at home, in Senath, Missouri July 3, 1953. At age 5 the family rented a small farm house on an active farm 40 miles southwest of St. Louis. While the family weren't farmers, they lived something of a homestead type life, raising a milk cow, sometimes two, and calves, a pig or two, chickens, and the occasional goat. Along with the stock, a large garden helped to feed Jerry's three brothers and two sisters for several years. Fishing and hunting contributed to the pantry, as did foraging the wild edibles on the property.

At the age of 14, the family, minus a brother and two sisters that were now adults and on their own, moved back to Senath. Having been encouraged from an early age to read, Jerry was a regular patron of the Senath Branch Library.

A love of a good story was born within him, and shortly before graduating high school, for a lack of stories that he liked at the library, he began to write short vignettes, and started taking notes for stories that he wanted to tell. Jerry eventually began to write in earnest and now has more than 100 titles to his credit including Prep/PAW stories, Action/Adventure, and a few of the romance type stories that first got him started.

9 780692 590355